"We'll take it slow."

Michael stretched and added, "You don't want to overdo it—although you *are* in great shape."

His smile warmed Allie right down to her toes. She didn't know where or when, but she was certain, as sure as God had made Cheerios, that Michael Rhodes was going to make love to her again. Lord, she hoped it would be soon.

"Want to warm up first?" he panted, jogging in place.

"No. I think I've done that already." Just watching him made her heart pump faster.

"C'mon, then. To the marina and back."

"All the way to the marina? That'll take half the morning!"

"Well . . ." He ran a semicircle around her and headed for the house. "There are other ways to exercise." He leered charmingly. "Follow me, and I'll show you what I have in mind. . . ."

Kristine Rolofson lives in Hope, Idaho—population one hundred seventy-three. She chose this beautiful setting for her first book, and when Harlequin bought the manuscript, Kristine says the whole town helped her celebrate.

Born in South Carolina, the daughter of a Navy chief, Kristine grew up in Rhode Island, where she ultimately met her husband, Glen. A bookworm then—and now—she recalls spending many nights reading under the blankets by flashlight. Five years ago, with a borrowed typewriter, two of her three children in diapers and a wallpaper-hanging business to run, Kristine began writing. The result? *One of the Family*, an exceptional first novel.

One of the Family

KRISTINE ROLOFSON

Harlequin Books

TORONTO • NEW YORK • LONDON
AMSTERDAM • PARIS • SYDNEY • HAMBURG
STOCKHOLM • ATHENS • TOKYO • MILAN

Published November 1987

ISBN 0-373-25279-X

Printed in Canada

1

"BE GOOD, NOW. I'll be right back." Allie sternly eyed the two small children squirming on the front seat of the battered blue pickup. They grinned back at her, one pair of green eyes and one pair of brown eyes shining with customary mischief.

"We will!" they chorused, and Allie's expression softened. She knew they were tired and sandy, but their afternoon at the lake had been worth it. The children glowed with sunlit good health. It had been a long winter in north Idaho, filled with snow and too much rain, and Allie meant to enjoy every sunny day the summer had to offer. Even if it meant she had to stay up half the night working to make up for the time lost.

She opened the door and stepped onto the paved slope that served as a parking area.

"Watch your fingers!" she cautioned before shutting the door of the truck and, after a final warning smile, walked toward the small cement-block post office to pick up her mail.

Allie was a summer person. At least she thought so on hot July days such as this one, when the lake sparkled like blue glass shining against its mountain backdrop. A warm breeze lifted her bangs from her forehead and ruffled the curling tips of her long hair as she walked up to the small sidewalk. She swung the heavy glass door open and stepped inside, blinking to adjust to the dim, cool interior of the post office.

"Afternoon, Al!" called a familiar voice behind the counter. "Hot enough for you today?"

"It sure is, Jim," she answered, her quick smile flashing across a wide counter toward the room where she knew the gray-haired man would be—at his desk now, finishing up whatever paperwork a postmaster has to have done before Friday's closing time.

But her smile was blocked by the broad back of a man, a very large figure in a T-shirt and shorts who leaned casually against the counter, a bright orange cycling helmet dangling loosely from one hand. Another tourist, she thought, dismissing him—until he turned to face her and she saw his eyes. They were a warm chocolate-brown color that reminded her of Hershey bars and Sherry's teddy bear.

But when she blinked again she realized this was no teddy bear. He was definitely better looking than the ragged toy her daughter dragged through the house. And he was much bigger. His broad shoulders filled up half the space available between the wall and the postal scale. Dark hair curled damply around his ears and temples, and sunburn highlighted his very handsome nose. There was open curiosity in his gaze, and something in his expression that made Allie glad she had pulled a somewhat sandy, oversize T-shirt over her striped bikini, even if it did say, "Welcome to Idaho. Set your clock back 25 years."

She quickly turned away before she embarrassed herself by staring any longer. She stepped in front of the wall of mailboxes, suddenly grateful to have something else to do besides gawk at a gorgeous tourist who was probably lost. With the experience born of two years of practice, she turned the dial on her combination lock. It was one of many small-town rituals she enjoyed.

She could hear Jim explaining the difference between the old highway and the new one. The door to her mailbox swung open and she reached inside, hoping to find something more than bills. Optimist, she chided herself, as she pulled out a supermarket flyer, the telephone bill, an offer to sell a set of luggage for "only" $79.99, and one thick cream-colored envelope. No surprise there; she'd helped Jeanne address her wedding invitations just a few days ago.

"Head east about five hundred yards until you cross the tracks, turn right till the stop sign, then you're back on the highway. You can't miss it." Jim was in his glory giving directions.

The dark-haired man murmured something in a low questioning voice as Allie gathered the mail into a bundle and turned to leave.

"Wait a minute, Al," called the elderly postmaster. "This gentleman is looking for a place to spend the night. Is Samowen full, do you know?"

She glanced over to the two men. Jim stood across the counter opposite the stranger, a hopeful expression on his kind face. The man with the warm brown eyes looked at her as if he thought she might impart some kind of wisdom he'd be interested in hearing. He raised one dark eyebrow as he repeated, a question in his deep voice, "Samowen?"

"That's the Forest Service campground nearby," she explained. "But I just came from there, and it looked like they were turning people away. It fills up fast on the weekends."

He obviously thought she knew what she was talking about, because he directed his next question to her. "Are there any other places to stay around here?"

"Well, there are several resorts right on the lake, here in Hope, but they're probably full. It's the busy season."

"Oh, well, I guess I'll just have to get back on the highway and keep trying. Thanks for the information."

She noted he looked hot and sweaty, but it only gave him an athletic sort of glow that radiated male sex appeal. When he smiled she returned it, absently brushing back strands of damp auburn hair that hung past her shoulders and blaming her warmly flushed skin on too much exposure to the strong afternoon sun.

"Well, good luck," she said, feeling somehow as if she'd let him down. But an outdoors type such as he appeared to be must be used to camping on the side of the road, probably even thrived on it, she told herself.

She ducked her head against the glare of the sunshine as she pushed open the door, her thoughts turning to dinner. The market next door carried her favorite brand of frozen pizza, but she was sure she had a package of hot dogs somewhere in the refrigerator. There were only a few hours left before Jeanne's party, and she would have to make the most of every minute before her guests arrived. It had been crazy to take the kids swimming when she had company coming tonight, but Allie hadn't been able to resist their pleas. And she had wanted to wear them out so they would go to sleep quickly and not be underfoot. She turned toward her truck, deciding to go straight home.

She stopped short in disbelief, her frantic glance sweeping the small parking area. Her truck wasn't there. Jim's Subaru was in its usual spot against the stone wall but her truck was not. The children! Where were the children?

"My truck's gone!" she cried out, but there was no one to hear. The sound of a crying child could be heard over Allie's pounding heartbeat, which had filled her ears with roaring panic. Allie shaded her eyes with one shaking hand and found the source of the weeping. Past the parking area, down the small incline to the road, across the street, sat her truck.

Allie ran as fast as she could.

"Glen! Sherry! Are you all right?" Their frightened little faces were streaked with tears. Allie wrenched open the door and leaned inside. "Are you okay, sweetie?" she asked, gathering her daughter's trembling body into her arms and peering past her to Glen. Glen's green eyes were wide in his heart-shaped face.

"It m-m-moved and it wouldn't sto-o-p!" Sherry sobbed.

"Sh-h-h, honey, it's okay. What happened, Glen?" she asked her son, realizing Sherry was too upset to make any sense at all.

"We were wrestling," he whispered.

"And?" she prompted. A sneaking suspicion wiggled into Allie's brain, and she could almost guess the rest.

"We hit that thing, I think—" he pointed toward the stick shift "—and then we started moving."

"Haven't I told you *never* to touch anything in the car?"

He nodded, his eyes brimming with unshed tears.

"You could have been killed." Suddenly the danger of the situation made Allie's knees grow weak. What if a car had been coming when they crossed the road, or what if they had tried to jump out of the moving truck or . . . She took a deep shuddering breath to dispel the flashing images of tragedy as she gathered the children into her arms and hugged them tightly against her.

"I'm sorry, Mommy!" wailed Glen, his face pale.

"It's okay, honey," she reassured him as she patted his back through his Superman T-shirt. "There's no harm done."

"I wouldn't be too sure about that," said a grim male voice behind her.

What now? she wondered. Releasing the children, she backed out of the truck. When she turned she saw the stranger from the post office, frowning toward the tail end of the truck. "Excuse me?"

"Here's your mail. You dropped it on the sidewalk. Are the kids okay?"

She thought it was awfully nice of him to be so concerned. "Thank you." She smiled politely, taking the envelopes he handed her. "They're not hurt, thank goodness."

"Good." The relief in his voice was sincere, but he looked at her as if she was not quite sane. "I parked my bike here," he explained carefully, "in the shade." He gestured toward the cool shadows of the maple trees that framed the town's only historical marker.

Allie stared apprehensively past the truck's bumper.

"Did we . . . did the truck—?" she stammered.

He nodded. "You guessed it, lady."

As she followed him around to the back of the truck, Allie's first thought was that the ladies of the Hope Garden Club were not going to be pleased. Colorful zinnias, pansies and snapdragons had survived a rainy Idaho spring only to lie crushed under the worn rear tires of her blue Datsun. The monument, a tribute to the Garden Club's generosity, was undamaged and still proclaimed the honor the area's residents felt in their town's beginnings as an Indian trading post. A silver bike lay trapped between the granite marker and the truck. Allie quickly stopped wondering what the Garden Club was going to say and started worrying about the mangled bicycle and its grim-looking owner.

"Oh, no," she breathed, turning to face the overpoweringly large man beside her. She was at eye level with his T-shirt, close enough to notice the curling chest hair that tickled its faded green neckline. She pulled her eyes to his face, past the strong angles of jaw and cheekbone to the shadowed eyes that surveyed the damage for which she was responsible. His eyebrows drew together in a worried frown. Handsome, Allie affirmed, but definitely grim.

"I'm really sorry," she said, finding the words inadequate as soon as they were out of her mouth.

"Not as much as I am."

There was a brief silence. "I have insurance," she offered meekly.

"So do I, but that's not going to help much right now." He absentmindedly ran one very large bronze paw through his thick hair, the silver highlights glinting attractively in the sunlight that filtered down between the maple leaves.

"Look, my insurance will pay for a new bike." At least she certainly hoped so. She glanced at her watch. Almost five o'clock. Probably too late to call her insurance company, but she'd try anyway. Maybe they had an emergency number.

"This is—was—a custom-made bicycle."

Allie sighed. Great. A custom-made bicycle. Where was she going to find one of those? "Maybe I can have it repaired?"

He smiled slightly. "It's possible, but I doubt it. What happened here anyway?"

She glanced back at the truck, and saw the children staring out the back window. Their fear had obviously been replaced by curiosity. She gestured toward them. "They were roughhousing and hit the gearshift. The slope was enough to start the truck rolling and it didn't stop until it hit—" Allie hesitated, and gestured toward the crumpled metal "—your custom bicycle."

"Emergency brake?"

"Worn out."

He sighed. "I don't suppose there's any kind of repair shop nearby?"

She shook her head. "Not for bikes, but what about one of the marinas?" she asked hopefully. Positively brilliant thinking, she congratulated herself. "There are mechanics there."

He looked at her with new respect. "Sounds worth a try. Would you mind giving us a lift?"

"It's the least I can do." She felt flustered and embarrassed. She should have suggested that herself. What on earth was the matter with her?

She hopped up on the truck's bumper and rearranged the rubber raft, air mattresses and picnic basket. The "tourist," as Allie thought of him, easily lifted the bike over the tailgate. He arranged several bright blue nylon packs around the bicycle, and then, almost as an afterthought, threw in the helmet he had been holding.

"I am really sorry about this," she told him when he stepped away from the truck. She jumped off the edge of the tailgate and motioned him toward the passenger door. "Hop in."

She opened the truck door and slid onto the sticky vinyl seat. "Move over, kids, and let—" She realized she didn't know his name.

"Michael," he supplied through the open window before he opened the door.

"And let Michael in," she finished, tossing her mail on the dashboard. "And behave yourselves. You've caused enough trouble for one day as it is." She knew they realized the man's bike was broken, but if they hadn't figured out their connection to the incident she would explain it to them tonight, privately. Right now she had to get this man's bike fixed.

"Can I sit on your lap?" asked Sherry. Her rich dark curls stuck damply to her neck, which looked too tired to hold up her head any longer. The front of the pickup was small to begin with, but it seemed to have shrunk to half its size with Michael in the front seat. His strong brown thighs took up most of the space to the right of the gear-shift.

She heard him say "Sure," in answer to Sherry's question, and Glen scrunched up his legs so Allie would be able to shift. She reached toward the ignition.

"Glen, where are they?"

He slowly pulled the ring of keys from behind his back.

The choking sound from her new passenger could have been interpreted as laughter or frustration. Allie figured it had to be the latter, and grabbed the keys quickly. She didn't look at Michael as she explained, "Glen's had some kind of attraction to keys since he was little. I usually don't leave them around where he can get at them, but I was in a hurry to get home today."

"How old are you, Glen?" Michael questioned. Sherry's head of tousled curls was snuggled into his shoulder.

"I'm six, Sherry's three and Mom's twenty-nine. How old are you?"

"Thirty-eight."

Allie slid the key into the ignition and started the engine. "I hope nothing's wrong with the tires," she muttered to herself.

"There didn't seem to be," answered Michael.

She swung the truck onto the quiet road. Allie wasn't surprised no one else had witnessed the accident. There was no traffic now, not uncommon for a hot Friday afternoon when people were usually still out on the lake fishing or at the beach where it was cool. Jim had the mail distributed by eleven o'clock in the morning, which was the time when most people went to the post office and gathered to exchange a little local gossip.

They passed the market and the elementary school, an old two-story brick building whose windows faced the gleaming lake, before turning right onto the access road that crossed the railroad tracks and connected the old highway with the new one.

Allie felt hot, sandy and completely unattractive. She hoped Michael was a nice normal person and not some sort of cycling pervert who conned naive women into picking him up. The ludicrous thought made her smile to herself as she reminded her overactive imagination just exactly how much she and her family were to blame for this situation.

"That's a big lake," commented Michael. "It seems like I've been riding within sight of it for hours."

"This is just one end of it, called Ellisport Bay. There are a couple of marinas and several resorts, too. It's a popular place, especially in the summertime."

She turned the truck onto the highway and passed several resorts, their No Vacancy signs a reminder of her words at the post office.

"Keep your fingers crossed," she told him as she pulled into the marina's dirt driveway. But crossed fingers didn't help, for when Allie returned to Michael and the drowsy children, she shook her head. "There's no one around here that knows much about bicycles, I'm afraid. Chris—the mechanic—recommended taking it in to Sandpoint tomorrow."

He frowned. "I think I came through there this afternoon. About twenty miles southwest of here?"

She nodded. "It's our closest town. I'll be happy to drive you in the morning."

"Thanks. But I don't have much hope that it can be repaired. I don't suppose there's any place to rent a car around here?"

"The nearest place is the airport in Spokane, and that's a hundred miles away."

"I know."

Of course. He had probably cycled through there. By the time Allie started the truck and headed back down the highway and into Hope again, she was satisfied that Michael was not going to kidnap her children or steal her truck. He'd have to be crazy to steal this old thing—it was rapidly becoming an eyesore.

But now what was she going to do with him? Thanks to her children, he was without transportation in a tiny town full of tourists. He had no place to stay, which wasn't exactly her fault, since he had been in that position when she'd first seen him. But still . . . there was a feeling of responsibility she just couldn't shake. It *was* her fault that he couldn't pedal down the road to another town, not that there were that many between here and Missoula, the direction he'd been heading, which was another two hundred miles east. Should she take him back to Sandpoint tonight? She crossed that option off the list when she realized there was no guarantee he'd find a room there, either. Why should she be so worried? He looked like a man who could take care of himself. Could he sue her? She'd have to find out. But for now . . .

Her stomach rolled emptily, reminding her that it was a long time since she'd eaten an avocado and sprout sandwich on the beach at noon. She glanced at Michael, so patiently holding Sherry in his big brown arms.

"Are you hungry?" She swung the car up the one-lane paved road that sliced through East Hope.

"Yes," he admitted and finally smiled, reaching up to his cheek to release a sticky tendril of Sherry's hair. "Look, uh, Alice..." He hesitated as if he wasn't sure he had remembered her name correctly. "Would you drop me off at that market? There was a phone booth in front of it and I need to make a few calls. I still don't have a place to stay tonight."

Allie guided the little truck past the well-cared-for homes on the quiet residential street and into a gravel parking area in front of a weather-beaten garage.

"Yay! We're home!" Glen cried, making Sherry open her eyes and yawn.

"You can make your calls from here, my house. I'll fix all of us something to eat. I'm really sorry about everything."

"We'll figure it out, don't worry," he assured her as he slid out of the truck and helped Sherry climb down. "I've never seen a garage like that."

"What?" She didn't know what was so different about the shingled building, except that it looked as if it might collapse during the next snowstorm.

"All the antlers. Your husband must be quite a hunter."

She looked above the wooden sliding doors to the deer and elk racks that decorated the garage's wooden eaves. "No, they came with the place when I bought it. Pretty rustic, huh?"

"We don't *have* a daddy," supplied Glen in a very matter-of-fact tone.

Michael looked confusedly at Glen, not knowing how to respond to such a blunt statement from the small boy. Then dark eyebrows tilted questioningly at Allie above piercing eyes. "Oh?"

"I'm divorced." She looked away from him when she said it. How she hated that word.

"I'm sorry." There was a curious echo of understanding in his words. She suddenly wondered if he was married, which wasn't likely, considering the solitary way he chose to spend his summer.

"Don't be. I'm not." The words came out stiffer than she intended. To soften her rudeness she added, "The children miss their father. He lives in Anchorage." With the waitress he had taken to Alaska with him, she added silently. She was just thankful Paul hadn't wanted even partial custody of the children.

She turned and left all the stuff in the back of the truck. First things first, she thought. And one of those things was to call her insurance company. Then get some food on the table, see if she could find Michael a place to stay, and track down Danny. He should be back from the beach by now.

She took the cement steps down to the back door two at a time, swinging open the screen door to the entryway. Her kitchen was always cool and dark in the afternoons. The square, two-story white house had a certain old-fashioned charm. She'd moved into the place after the divorce, and she'd liked its shabby comfort from the first time she'd seen it. There were newer and more elegant homes on the two streets that made up the town, but she preferred living in one of the small, older models. The yard would need a team of gardeners to make it look presentable, but there was nothing wrong with Big Wheel tracks instead of perfect lawn, and sandboxes where gardens should be.

Michael had stopped halfway down the steps to admire the ramshackle playhouse Glen was proudly pointing out. Allie, pausing inside the kitchen door, had time to admire Michael.

He was a large man, not overweight, but with a certain solidness that belied the easy grace he displayed. He was very tan, and the hair on his legs made him look even darker. The faded green T-shirt hung in a baggy wave past his waist. His square face was handsome, strong, and the silver touches that swept through his thick, curling hair made Allie wonder why on earth a grown man didn't have better things to do than pedal around the highways like some college freshman.

He looked toward the back door and caught Allie watching him. His questioning glance held hers for a split second before she opened the screen door and said, "Come on in."

Michael entered the house almost warily, letting his eyes adjust to the dim interior. She wondered uncomfortably if he was having doubts about what he'd gotten himself into. *Well, that makes two of us,* she agreed silently.

Michael looked around the kitchen, his glance taking in the blue cupboards, yellow counter and patterned quilted wallpaper that stretched the length of the narrow room. The hardwood floor gleamed underneath his scruffy tennis shoes. The kitchen was clean, thank goodness, because with this recent heat wave she hadn't done much cooking.

"Let me get something cold for us to drink and then I'll make a few calls, see if I can get you a place to stay. And... Damn!"

"What?"

"I didn't know how late it was." The microwave's digital clock blinked its numbers at her. She would have to make every minute count if she was to be ready for tonight's festivities.

"Looks like you're having a party." He peered into the living room at the pink and yellow crepe paper streamers that radiated from a small brass chandelier to the corners of the room.

"A wedding shower. It looks pretty, doesn't it?" She was glad she had awakened early and tackled the dust and vacuumed the slate-blue carpet before the summer sun poured into the south windows. At least one room in the house was ready for a party.

"*Your* wedding shower?"

"Oh, no!" she corrected with a small laugh. "A good friend of mine is getting married in a couple of weeks. We're having a party tonight to celebrate." She pulled the telephone book out of a narrow drawer by the phone and looked up a number. Before she dialed, she said, "There's iced tea and beer in the fridge—help yourself."

"Thanks," he replied, moving to the refrigerator and opening the door. He bent over to look inside and with a satisfied "Ah" pulled out a frosty can of beer.

Allie wasn't surprised that no one answered at the insurance office at this hour. But what was she going to do? She had never hit anybody before—hadn't had any accidents at all—and she really didn't know the extent of her responsibilities. She was sure taking her victim home with her was not part of the scenario.

"There's no answer. I'll have to try them again on Monday." She hung up the phone, reluctant to spend the weekend wondering how to resolve her predicament.

"I'll call mine instead," Michael offered calmly.

He certainly didn't seem very worried. If this had happened to her, she'd be a basket case. But nothing like this would ever happen to Allie Leonard because, she thought wryly, she'd never been alone for more than a few minutes at a time in her whole life. How could she ever be stranded in the middle of nowhere? Three children would have wailed, "Mom, what are we going to *do*?"

Three children. Danny. "Excuse me, please." She picked
up the phone again and dialed a well-memorized number.
When Barbara answered, Allie said, "Hi, it's me."

"Hi! We just got back from the beach a few minutes ago.
I would have sent Dan home, but there was no answer
when he called. You must have stopped at the store."

"No, I just picked up my mail." And a pile of trouble,
she longed to add, just to hear her friend's response, but
she didn't dare. Michael was still standing by the refrigerator and could hear every word she said.

"You sound mysterious. Are you all set for tonight?"

"Just fine, if everyone comes late. I seem to be running
out of time."

"Want me to come early? Ron's already home, working
out in the garden. I'll throw some sandwiches on the table
for them and come over as soon as I can."

"Don't hurry, really. I haven't even fixed dinner yet. But
don't forget the huckleberry sauce for the cheesecake. And
thanks for bringing Dan home."

"No problem. See you in a little while."

Allie hung up the phone and leaned against the yellow
counter, unsure suddenly. Her house felt almost invaded,
and she didn't like being in the position of having a
stranger inside the cozy haven she'd created for her children.

Glen slammed the screen door, announcing his arrival
to the world. "Dan's home!" he called.

"Who's Dan?" Michael asked.

"My oldest son."

"How many kids do you have?" She couldn't help no-
ticing how he quickly inspected her trim figure.

"Just the three." Understatement of the summer.

"Hi, Mom, I'm starved! What's for dinner?" A lanky
boy with shaggy cinnamon hair bounded into the kitchen,
his freckled face sporting a peeling sunburned nose.

"Just a minute, Danny. I'd like you to meet Michael. Uh, we, uh, met him this afternoon after the truck ran over his bike."

"Tell me you're kidding, Mom," said her ten-year-old son. He gazed up at Michael with the respect a bony kid has for giant, muscular men.

"No kidding," she sighed. "Michael, if you want to use the phone, there's an extension in the sewing room where you'll have some peace and quiet."

"Fine." He followed her down a hall, past the bathroom and into a cluttered room that held a desk, shelves and the odds and ends no one had room for. It had started out to be a sewing room until Allie had found it more comfortable to sew on the large oak table in the living room.

"Here you go," Allie said, removing a stack of quilting magazines from the desk chair.

She turned away, shut the door firmly behind her, then made her way down the hall and back into the kitchen. "Where's Sherry?" she asked the boys, who were rummaging through the cracker box eating saltines. "And get out of there. You'll ruin your supper."

"Out in the playhouse, I think," Glen answered.

"Glen, go in the bathroom and get ready for a bath." She ignored his groan and looked at Danny, who was still wearing his swimsuit and looking pretty sandy around the edges. "You, too, Dan. In fact, both of you get in the shower together while I figure out something for dinner."

They each stuffed another cracker in their mouths before running down the hall. The bathroom door slammed shut and soon giggling and running water could be heard through the walls. She hoped Michael didn't need or expect total quiet for his conversation. There was no such thing in this house. She opened the freezer door of the refrigerator and searched for the package of hot dogs until she found them under some frozen french fries. This was her idea of summertime cooking. Winters were for home-made bread and thick stews that simmered all day on the stove. But summer was for fun, which meant you didn't stay inside cooking all afternoon when you could be at the beach. She put some water in the microwave for a fresh batch of iced tea, then rummaged through the cupboard for a box of potato chips.

She didn't hear Michael come back into the room until he said, "I'm finished with the phone now. I had to leave a message with a friend who'll call me back. He might be able to ship me another bike."

"But I don't think I'll be able to reach my insurance agent until Monday." Which could make for a very long week-end, she worried.

"Well, I guess I stay in Hope until Monday, then. Actually, it looks like a beautiful place. I won't mind the extra days here." He looked past her into the living room, where a view of the lake shimmered beyond the sliding glass doors.

"But you don't have a place to stay," Allie protested, then realized what she'd said as the words popped from her mouth.

"All I need is a spot to set up my tent." His meaning was clear.

Allie was silent. She did not want this man camped in her yard.

"And I noticed," he continued, "you have a very large tree with a perfect spot for a tent underneath it."

She shook her head slowly. "I'll make a few calls, see if there's anything else available."

"Fine. In the meantime, I've left your number where I can be reached, and I'll need to take those calls person-ally."

"Well—"

"Lady, you don't have much choice. I think I've been damn patient with this whole situation. You've destroyed a very valuable bike and set me back Lord knows how many days on my trip. Not to mention the inconvenience!"

"Uh, do you like hot dogs?"

He grinned, the white teeth emphasizing his smile, the deep laugh lines etched in his face. "My favorite." He turned and strode toward the door. "I'll go get my gear set up."

The bathroom door flew open. Danny ran after him eagerly, calling, "Can I help? I know a good spot—" Glen followed him. Dan's voice trailed off as the door banged shut. Allie sighed. There was no mistaking the enthusiasm the boys felt at having a man in the house. They were like eager little puppies lapping up attention.

I don't need this in my life. She sighed. Everything was perfectly fine before now, before today. It was bad enough to feel responsible for a stranger's welfare, but to have the children become too attached to him would be a disaster. He would be on his way pedaling a new bike in a matter of a day or two.

She unwrapped the package of hot dogs and grabbed a pot from the hanging hook above the stove. She filled it with water, submerging the frozen brick of hot dogs, trying to separate them. Their gray mass floated to the top of the water and Allie thought she'd never seen anything so unappetizing in her life. Well, at least it was food, and there was probably a can of beans in the cupboard, too. She set the pan on the stove, turned the burner to high, and then realized she was still in her bathing suit. It had begun to itch.

She peered out the kitchen window. Michael had obviously gone up to the truck to get his packs. How long did it take to pitch a tent? Or better yet—how long did it take to dismantle one? He had better not plan on making himself too comfortable. One of her guests tonight owned a resort. There had to be someplace else she could send him.

2

MICHAEL LIFTED HIS PACKS out of the truck bed and handed them to the waiting boys. "Why don't you put these under the tree and then we'll get the tent set up."

"Right," the older boy agreed importantly. "C'mon, Glen." The younger child, the one with his mother's green eyes, shot Michael a happy grin, then followed his brother down the steps. Michael found himself smiling back before he turned to the truck and lifted the ruined bicycle over its side. He leaned it against the shack Alice called a garage and wondered what in hell he had gotten himself into. The boys seemed like good enough kids, though the worship in their eyes made him a little uncomfortable. He was used to boys. But the little girl reminded him of things he'd spent the past three years trying to forget. Once he made it through this trip to Montana he planned to bury the past for good. And it was about time, too.

Michael stepped away from the garage and looked toward the house. He shoved his hands in his pockets and watched the boys move a bulky plastic scooter out from under the tree. The yard was a mess, he noted, but the house was comfortable. It felt like a place a man could look forward to coming home to. Which might have something to do with the pretty woman *inside* the house, he added with a silent chuckle. Not that he had time for a green-eyed lady with a dancer's legs, he reminded himself as he walked down the steps. But he had to admire her spunk. She hadn't pulled that "helpless female" routine he detested, but he knew she'd been upset. Alice had the kind of face that couldn't hide her feelings. She didn't want him camped in her yard, and he could appreciate that. He liked his privacy, too. For the moment, though, neither one of them had any choice but to make the best of it.

"This is a good place," Danny told Michael as he approached. Michael looked where the boy pointed; it was a fairly level spot covered with shaded crabgrass.

"I think you're right," Michael agreed. "You boys want to give me a hand with the tent so we'll be finished before dinnertime?"

IN LESS THAN FIFTEEN MINUTES Allie had showered, taking the squirming Sherry into the tub with her for a quick rinse. She felt almost human again after she dried off and changed into clean khaki shorts and a flowered cotton shirt. Sherry demanded to choose her own outfit, and Allie left her in her bedroom to decide what that would be.

Allie's hair was wet but clean, and she had pulled it off her face with turquoise combs. She stayed barefoot, and pattered comfortably on the cool wood floor of the kitchen, peering out the window over the sink to see a bright orange tent in full bloom under her birch tree. She had the sinking feeling no one in the entire neighborhood could miss this tent, but she quickly reminded herself it was her fault to begin with. If she'd had that emergency brake fixed before now... But the estimate had been eighty dollars, and that wasn't exactly in her budget. She was lucky in many ways, she reminded herself. She had this house and the income each month from selling the land on the river. But her work barely covered the unbudgeted expenses, and Allie wasn't going to use her small savings account unless there was a real emergency.

The tent bulged suspiciously and moments later Danny and Glen emerged, their faces red from giggling. Allie loved seeing them laugh. Sherry, in clean play clothes and with a fresh burst of energy, couldn't bear to be left out and tumbled outside.

But where was Michael? Allie moved to the window over the kitchen table and saw him coming down the cement steps carrying a lumpy nylon bundle. He looked at the children. Allie heard him call to Sherry, who ran to him, and he swung her up in his big brown arms, hoisting her casually on his shoulders. With a shriek of joy she clutched her fingers into his mass of dark hair. He winced and reached to pry her fingers away with one hand, holding onto her chubby knee with the other. Allie sighed. They were quite a pair. It was painfully obvious how much Sherry needed a father.

"Hey, everybody, dinner's almost ready," she called from the back door.

"Here we go." Michael laughed as he swung Sherry off his shoulders in a whirl. She collapsed into a giggling heap on the grass. With a protectiveness he'd almost forgotten he possessed, Michael bent down to help her, gently lifting the child to her feet.

His expression was almost wistful, Allie thought. Did he have children of his own somewhere? A man who looked as good as he did certainly would have been married at some time in his life. She wondered what had happened, but then admonished herself—that was none of her business.

"Would you call the boys?" she asked when he carried Sherry to the door. Allie tried to sound casual, wincing a little at the cozy domestic conversation.

He straightened, his baggy green T-shirt surrounding his chest once again. "I'll go drag them out of the tent."

"Thanks."

Sherry walked importantly beside her new friend, chattering nonstop.

Allie loaded a tray with napkins, catsup, mustard and silverware and carried it past the table in the living room through the sliding glass door to the deck. The large picnic table there was a summer lifesaver.

"Can I give you a hand?" Michael asked when she returned to the kitchen. He had a feeling he made her nervous, but he certainly didn't have any idea why.

"No." She hadn't meant to sound so curt, but it had just come out that way. She wished he wouldn't stand quite so close; she wasn't used to anyone taking up so much room in her narrow kitchen. Allie forced a smile. "There isn't much to do, really."

"Have you lived here long, Mrs. Leonard?" he inquired politely. He stood next to her, watching as she fumbled through a tall cupboard. She made an intriguing picture as the cotton fabric of her blouse tightened against her breasts. He guessed what she was after and reached up easily, hauling out a plastic bag of paper plates. There was a light fragrance of flowers in her hair.

"Call me Allie." She took the package from his hand. "Since Sherry was a year old. And how do you know my last name?" She counted out five plates and put the rest back in the cupboard on a lower shelf.

"Your mail."

"What's yours?" She handed him the plates, figuring he might as well make himself useful.

"My what?" He frowned slightly, "Oh. Rhodes. Michael Rhodes."

"Nice to meet you, Mr. Rhodes." Allie had to smile at the sudden formality of the conversation. "Michael."

"My pleasure," he replied, and realized he meant it. He followed her out to the deck and sat down on the wooden bench with some difficulty. Certain tender parts of his anatomy were sore from unaccustomed hours on a bicycle seat. He shifted carefully and passed the paper plates around to the kids while Allie went back into the house for the rest of the food.

She wondered if there would be enough. He looked as if he could pack away quite a few pounds of it. Allie told herself the condition of Michael Rhodes's body was none of her business and tried to concentrate on dinner. She pulled a package of potato chips from a drawer and grabbed a wicker basket from its hook on the wall before dumping the chips unceremoniously into it. Paper cups would complete the picnic idea, and then she wouldn't have dishes. He wanted to stay; he would just have to take what was put in front of him. The beans bubbled in their saucepan on the stove, and she dumped them into a serving dish. In minutes the hot dogs were assembled, and she piled them onto another tray and took it out to the group waiting patiently for dinner.

"Yay, hot dogs!" cried Glen, his eyes gleaming behind the fringe of light brown bangs. *He needs a haircut*, she thought.

"Hot dogs again? We had those last night," complained Danny.

"And we may have them again tomorrow night," she teased him, "if you want me to spend all day at the beach."

She slid into the bench beside Dan, who faced Michael Rhodes man-to-man. Her bare knee brushed against Michael's briefly, and she adjusted her legs quickly to avoid more contact. The slight tingle only reminded her of her vulnerable position. Fortunately, he didn't seem as aware of her as she was of him. *I have to get out more. Even a blind date, if Jeanne offers to fix me up again.*

"Help yourself, please," she said politely. "Here, Sherry," she said, putting chips on her daughter's plate.

"Mmm . . . yum!"

There was a flurry of activity as the catsup and mustard and relish were passed from hand to hand. Suddenly it was quiet as everyone enjoyed the dinner.

"What do you eat when you bike around?" asked Dan, his cheeks bulging. "That dried fruit and stuff?" His Cub Scout camping trips had given him a taste of the outdoor life.

Michael shook his head. "I try not to. Most of the time I stop at fast food places and get hamburgers or pizza."

Dan's face fell. Obviously he had pictured a more independent outdoor existence. "Oh."

"But I have a small stove with me, in case I get stuck somewhere. I'll show you how it works if you want."

"Hey, neat!" Dan was relieved. His new hero might live up to his expectations after all. "Hey, Mom?"

"Mmm?" Her mouth was full.

"How did you wreck Michael's bike?"

Nosy kid. She swallowed without chewing. "Well, it wasn't easy."

"Mom!" he admonished, giving her a look that would freeze a goldfish dead in its bowl.

"Of course it was an accident, Dan, and we're all very sorry about it." She glanced meaningfully at the two younger children, who were sitting on either side of their guest.

"Sherry hit me—" Glen began to explain.

"Did not!"

"Did too," he replied automatically. "And I tickled her, just a little, and she kicked me, but she missed and I kicked her back and—"

"We get the picture." Allie tried to stem the flow of words. Reliving the crime was not her idea of scintillating dinner conversation.

"And that's when I think I kicked that stick," Glen finished as if he hadn't heard his mother.

"What stick?" asked Dan, fascinated.

"The gearshift." Michael filled in for him. "I think they knocked it into neutral—"

"And we rolled and rolled!" Sherry finished triumphantly, always happy to supply a punch line. She waved her hot dog like a rolling truck, grazing Michael's arm with catsup.

He absently picked up his napkin and wiped it off. "That's when they ran into my bike."

"Wow!" breathed Dan. "Were you riding it?"

Allie felt it was time she put an end to the conversation. "Mr. Rhodes was in the post office. He'd parked his bike by the monument, which is where the truck landed. And this is a serious matter, so listen, all of you." She took a deep breath, when she realized they were—all four of them—staring at her intently. "An expensive bicycle was ruined today. And Mr. Rhodes's trip has had to be delayed because of it. We are really sorry about what happened, aren't we?" She emphasized the last two words, and her younger children nodded in agreement.

"Oh, so berry sorry," sniffed Sherry, rubbing her mustard-smeared cheek on Michael's bare arm. "Never do it again, 'kay?"

Michael seemed speechless as he looked down at her. Allie had trouble keeping a straight face. She and the boys knew what Michael didn't: Sherry's angelic expression was just a cover for a personality made of pure steel.

"Mom, make her stop. This is embarrassing!" Dan whispered.

Allie shrugged, trying to hide her amusement. Big tough Michael Rhodes, for all his threats, was a lump of play dough as far as Sherry was concerned.

"Tiss me, tiss my Sherry," the little girl murmured.

"If you don't kiss her, she'll hit you," Glen advised, reaching for another handful of chips.

Michael patted her lightly on the top of her wispy dark curls and cleared his throat. "Eat your dinner now, okay? No one's mad about the bike anymore."

Allie raised an eyebrow at that. "Oh, no?"

"No," he said firmly. "You and I will work it out. Together."

Allie didn't have a suitable reply to that statement. They finished their dinner in silence, the kids effectively silenced by the guilt of their crime. When Allie asked Dan to clear the table he did so willingly.

"You want me to make coffee, Mom?" That was one of his after-dinner chores.

"Please, honey," she answered. She watched as Dan took Michael's plate. "Would you like coffee?" she asked.

"Yes. Thanks."

"Make a large pot, then, Dan," she said. "C'mon, kids, get this job done. We're having more company tonight." She looked at her watch. One hour and ten minutes to go until the party. She could have a cup of coffee with Michael and still have time to clean the downstairs bathroom.

The children slid off the benches and cleared the table while Michael and Allie sat quietly.

"They're nice kids," he said, surprising her.

"Thanks."

Silence.

"Do you have any children?" There was no ring on his finger, but that didn't mean anything these days.

He paused, as if deciding how to answer. "No," he said finally, and Allie had the impression that was a very hard thing for him to admit.

The tension made her uncomfortable, but she couldn't figure out why. There had been nothing harmful in the question. Maybe he just didn't like being asked about personal things. She would be better off keeping things on a strictly impersonal level.

He beat her to it. "You live in a beautiful place," he said, turning to admire the lake view from her deck.

"Where are you from, Michael?" It was natural to be curious, she told herself.

"Oregon."

When she realized he wasn't going to say anything else, she tried again. "And, uh, where were—are you going? Glacier Park? All the way across the country?"

He looked away from the lake and focused on the woman across from him. "Nothing so adventurous, I'm afraid." The explanation he'd given his friends and family came easily. "I planned to ride west and see some of the country until my time ran out, something I'd wanted to do since I was a kid."

He looked too young to be having a mid-life crisis, but Allie supposed it could happen to anyone at any time. "And now you're stuck here. I'll try to get you a cabin at one of the resorts if I can. And of course I'll pay for it," she added.

He frowned. "That's not necessary. I'm fine where I am." In fact, he realized, he was more than fine. And he wasn't going anywhere. Even if his bicycle was in perfect running order, he wasn't getting back on that seat right away.

Oh, you are, are you? She tried to remind herself he was actually a pretty good sport and she was the one behaving ungraciously. The reason he was here was all her fault in the first place. "Well, if you change your mind . . ."

"I won't." Then he smiled. "Besides, I think I'm going to enjoy myself here."

Here? Did he mean her backyard, or Hope, or the whole damn Northwest? The words sounded innocent enough, but the twinkle in his dark eyes caused heat to center in Allie's cheeks. "Here?" she echoed.

Dan carried two mugs of coffee across the deck and set them on the table. He looked disgusted. "Mom, Sherry and Glen ate all the leftover chips and now Sherry's licking the inside of the bag and making a mess."

"Call me when she starts eating the bag, Dan." Allie laughed at her son's expression. "Thanks for the coffee, honey, and I'll come inside in a minute."

Michael gestured toward the lake. "Great place for a vacation," he answered blandly.

"True. There's a lot to see."

He picked up the coffee mug and smiled at her, enjoying teasing her. Enjoying looking at her. "Yes. I read your T-shirt this afternoon."

She had to laugh. "Set your clock back twenty-five years?"

He nodded.

"It's really true," she insisted. "It's an old-fashioned way of life. Sometimes I think the saying should be, Set your clock back one hundred years." With his answering smile, she felt guilty for all the things she'd thought. He might be a little too stubborn for his own good, but he was solid and big and as comfortable on her deck as anyone had ever been. And he wouldn't last two days around her three kids. Somehow the thought cheered her.

"ALICE, DEAR, I just saw a man go into your bathroom." Lydia's concerned whisper carried above the murmur of conversation, which promptly stopped as ten women and one teenage girl looked at Lydia. "More wine, anyone?" she asked, unperturbed.

"There's a man *where*?" Barbara interrupted, holding out her empty glass to be filled. Her blue eyes twinkled with mischief.

"Oh, dear," murmured Lydia, a shy older woman with a sophisticated mixture of red and silver hair. "Maybe I shouldn't have said anything. But when I went into the kitchen to get the wine, there he was." She stopped, unwilling to call attention to herself any further.

"It's okay, Lyd," Allie assured her, trying to ease her friend's embarrassment. "Actually, I wanted to talk to you about that. Do you have any cabins available at the resort?" It was a long shot, but she had to try.

Lydia shook her head. "I've been turning away people for two weeks now. Sorry."

"Let's *all* talk about the man in your bathroom," teased Jeanne, with a wink at Barbara. She turned to Allie, who perched nervously on the arm of the navy-blue couch. "Are you having trouble with the plumbing again?"

"Not exactly." Allie stood, feigning a casual attitude. "Why don't you start opening presents now?"

"Not so fast," Barbara protested, holding up one hand. "I want to know more about this man. What does he look like? Is this something I can use in my column?"

"Not if you want to live to see forty-two," Allie joked, wishing someone would change the subject. She heard the shower running in the bathroom and hoped nobody else did. Michael certainly seemed to know how to make himself at home.

Lydia looked uncomfortable. "I thought he was very good looking. Red or white?" she asked, holding up a carafe.

"The white you have there is fine," Barbara said. "You really should loosen up a bit, Al. No one cares if you have a man around. In fact, we would all celebrate for you." She nodded enthusiastically, her blond curls bouncing.

"In that case, Mom," drawled Christina, a good-natured fifteen-year-old, "I think I should celebrate with something stronger than diet cola."

"Is anyone ready for cheesecake and coffee?" A chorus of "no thank yous" filled the air. Allie scanned the vegetable trays and bowls of dip. Everyone had brought something to munch on, and it was enough so far. Maybe if they kept drinking wine they'd forget what they were talking about.

"C'mon, Jeanne, it's time." Allie handed her a stack of gaily wrapped packages. "That's what we're all here for."

Jeanne glowed. She set her wineglass on the coffee table and picked up a package and shook it. "Feels like pot holders."

Grace Farmin chuckled. "Open it quickly. I can't wait to see if you like it."

Allie perched on the edge of the sofa to watch. She and her friends were so happy for Jeanne. Bob was a sweetheart, and Allie just knew he and Jeanne were going to be great together.

Jeanne ripped off the silver paper and rustled through a layer of tissue paper to reveal a silky peach nightgown. "It's beautiful, Grace, thank you."

"I hope it fits. If not, feel free to exchange it for one that does," said her neighbor.

The nightgown was passed around among the group of admiring women, and the gift opening continued. All the packages contained sexy underwear and intimate lingerie. When Jeanne was finished, Grace sipped her iced tea and proclaimed, "That man of yours doesn't have a chance."

During a lull in the laughter, Jeanne, her green eyes dancing with mischief, leaned over to Allie and whispered, "Al, do you think he's finished in there by now?"

Allie choked a bit on her wine. "What are you talking about?"

"Do you think he's fixed the plumbing yet?"

"Who?"

"The plumber."

"Why don't you use the bathroom upstairs?"

"Good idea." She chuckled. "Unless you have men hidden all over the house. I'll be right back." Jeanne excused herself and left the room.

Barbara's eyes narrowed suspiciously. "He's not the plumber, is he?"

"Who'd like coffee? It's decaff," Allie called.

Three people nodded.

"Are you keeping something from us?" Barbara's voice was teasing. "Is that why there's a tent in your yard? I thought the boys were working on another Cub Scout badge."

"It's a long story," Allie hedged.

"Oh, good, I love long stories about men." Christina twirled a long dangly earring from one lobe and tried to look casual.

"Tina, keep still," Barbara admonished her daughter. "Don't make me sorry I let you come."

"Do you think he's still in there?" someone asked.

"I'll go see." Christina stood up eagerly.

"Stay right where you are." Barbara's command prompted a giggle from her daughter.

"I do need help with the cheesecake. Want to carry in the plates for me?"

"Okay. What's his name?" She followed Allie into the kitchen.

"Tina, I'd like you to meet Michael Rhodes." Allie was not surprised to see him talking to Jeanne and leaning against the counter as if he owned the place. Somehow she was surprised he hadn't sauntered into the living room and helped himself to the carrot sticks.

He smiled down at Tina. "Hi."

Allie felt sorry for the teenager. Michael looked as if he'd just stepped out of a television commercial, the kind brawny athletes make during their off-season. It was obvious he had just taken a shower. His wet hair, almost black, was brushed casually back from his forehead. A white T-shirt accentuated his muscular chest, and denim cutoffs exposed strong brown thighs. He was barefoot. Allie prayed he wouldn't go into the living room.

"Hi, I'm Tina Miller," she finally squeaked.

"Tina, would you get the cheesecake out of the refrigerator? Middle shelf." Allie remembered her manners. "Would you like some?" she asked him.

"No, thanks. Need help with anything?"

"I think I have everything under control."

"I'm sure you do," he drawled. Allie wasn't sure if that was meant as a compliment or not. Somehow it didn't sound like one.

"Excuse me," she said, waiting for him to move away from the silverware drawer so she could open it. She hesitated a moment, making sure his thighs were a safe distance from the handle before she reached to tug open the drawer.

"It was nice talking to you, Jeanne," he was saying. "I'll look forward to Sunday." He shoved his hands in his pockets and looked back at Allie. "By the way, where are the kids?"

"Upstairs, bribed with television programs and bags of M&Ms."

"Sounds like fun. Well, good night." He left the house quickly, but not before Allie sensed a certain loneliness about him.

"Nice man. Can I carry something in for you?" Jeanne looked pleased with herself. Her voice was a shade too casual, which didn't fool Allie for a minute.

"What did he mean about looking forward to Sunday?" There was an informal barbecue planned on the beach at the campground.

"I invited him to come along."

"Why?"

"Because, well, I was making conversation about camping and one thing led to another and pretty soon—"

"You invited him to the picnic," Allie finished.

"Sure." Jeanne shrugged.

"Sure," echoed Tina. "What a hunk. How did you meet him?"

"I picked him up when I got my mail."

"No kidding?" shrieked Tina.

"Cross my heart, kiddo," she answered. "The kids ran over his bike and wrecked it so he's staying here until I can get the insurance company to straighten out the mess."

"Then what?" She quit holding the pan the cheesecake was in and set it on the counter.

Allie glared at both of them. "Quit looking so excited. As soon as he gets a new bike he'll hop on it and ride away." She took the pan and the forks off the counter and started to go back into the living room. "And then," she said over her shoulder, "things will get back to normal around here."

MICHAEL STOOD OUTSIDE in the darkness for a long time before returning to his tent. The family life he'd suddenly been thrust into reminded him too much of the emptiness in his own. And of a need he hadn't known he had. He could get out first thing in the morning, if he wanted to— rent a car from somewhere or buy an inexpensive ten-speed in town.

But there wasn't any hurry, he told himself as he opened the tent. He was close enough, and a few extra days weren't going to make any difference one way or another. Michael slipped into the sleeping bag, grateful for the warmth now that the evening had grown cool. The hot shower had eased some of the aches and pains he'd accumulated on the trip, but it sure felt good to lie down. He chuckled, thinking about the woman he'd surprised in the kitchen, the one who'd invited him to a picnic. Obviously Allie Leonard didn't have men walking around her house often. And she wasn't pleased about it now. He could tell. But he wasn't going anywhere. Not until he was good and ready. And if Allie Leonard expected him to camp on the side of the road like some damn hobo, she was in for a surprise.

3

"THAT'S RIGHT, make it burn..." Jane Fonda's voice urged from the small cassette recorder on the coffee table.

"It's burning, it's burning," panted Allie, her head bent over toward the floor while she stretched her muscles in her calves. It was almost over. It just had to be. Vanity, she thought, making her torture herself at six o'clock every morning. But that was the only time of day the house was ever truly quiet. Sometimes Glen, who was an early riser, would curl up at the end of the couch and watch television with the sound turned off until she'd finished, but even he was sleeping a little late this morning. All the excitement of yesterday must have taken its toll.

Allie yawned, wishing she could still be snuggled under the covers, too. But a cup of coffee and a hot shower would be the next best thing, she decided, feeling the trickles of perspiration between her small breasts.

She was in the middle of the last cool-down stretches when she heard the back door open. For a second she was startled until she remembered she had a guest. Michael. Who could forget him?

"Breathe deeply, relax, relax..." crooned the recorded voice.

Allie had to smile. How could Jane be so smart?

"So that's your secret."

She stretched upward with one long graceful movement to face him. He leaned against the kitchen doorjamb, practically filling the entrance. He wore jogging shorts that had obviously been used over several thousand miles, and the green T-shirt he'd had on yesterday was ringed in sweat. His face was wet, as if he'd dunked it under the outside faucet. He was all male, Allie noted, and her stretched muscles contracted painfully before she forced herself to relax. She could feel fresh pulses of awareness as the blood pumped steadily through her heated body.

"What secret?" She was suddenly uncomfortable and not just a little grumpy. She didn't like to talk so early in the morning, especially not to a half-dressed giant who was staring at her body. She plucked the damp material of her shirt away from her chest. Damn—she never wore a bra when she exercised! She leaned over to switch off the now-silent tape, wishing her sweatpants didn't look as though two more people could fit into them with her.

"Why you're in such good shape. You do this every morning?"

She let the compliment slide by, hoping the red in her face would be mistaken for overexertion. She pressed the rewind button. "I try to, except on Sundays." She wanted to go into the kitchen and pour herself a cup of coffee. She wanted to savor every luxurious quiet moment. She did not want to make small talk.

"And what do you do on Sundays?"

She glanced up at him, wondering if he was teasing her. She decided he was just trying to make conversation. Okay, she might as well be polite. "Stay in bed and eat doughnuts," she replied. She waited for the tape to shut itself off as her breathing came back to normal.

"All by yourself?" For a second he'd thought she was kidding. He hadn't met very many women he'd liked well enough to spend Sunday morning with. And eating doughnuts hadn't been part of the plan, either.

"None of your business." She smiled, watching him frown. "Actually, no," she relented. "With three kids. It's pretty messy, but we spend a lot of winter Sundays that way."

"You have any other vices?" he asked good-naturedly. She had a sense of humor when she relaxed, he noted. He liked the way she looked, too. Natural. There was an energy inside of her he wouldn't mind exploring if circumstances were different.

She shook her head. "Nope." She yanked the cord out of the wall and wound it around the recorder, then pushed the coffee table back into place in front of the battered blue couch. "You've been running. You do that every morning?"

"Try to," he echoed, his dark eyes twinkling. "Except on Sundays."

"And what do *you* do on Sundays?" When she stepped toward him, he backed out of the doorway to let her into the kitchen. She took two blue mugs from the cupboard beside the white porcelain sink.

"Stay in bed. Watch football on TV." He took the empty cup she handed him and reached for the coffeepot. Michael waited for her to ask the next part of the question, but she didn't, to his amusement. He filled their cups and replaced the glass carafe. "But I'll have to try your way sometime." He pushed aside the intriguing vision of doughnut crumbs against Allie's smooth skin.

"Where'd you go?" Not exactly original conversation, but what could he expect at six in the morning? When she swallowed, the hot liquid made a delicious burning trail down her throat.

"Just around Hope."

"There are only two streets. It couldn't have been much of a run."

"I went around more than once. I think I have the houses practically memorized by now. It's a beautiful day," he noted, as the sunshine streamed through the uncurtained window above the sink.

He looked perfectly at home leaning casually against the counter. For a moment she wished she was one of those women who wore beautiful robes and had their hair tied neatly back and their makeup on first thing in the morning. But she didn't think her children would appreciate the effort.

She looked past Michael to see her sleepy little son, dragging his blanket behind him, headed toward her. She hadn't heard him come down the stairs. "Hello, Glen," she said softly.

She kissed the top of his head, inhaling the sweet smell of him. "Why don't you go watch *Sesame Street* while I have a shower. Then I'll fix breakfast. Okay?"

He nodded obediently and disappeared around the corner.

"I think he's walking in his sleep. He's a cute kid, Allie."

"Thanks." Allie noted a certain wistfulness in his eyes as she studied him silently. He was a mystery to her, yet somehow she felt comfortable having him around. Well, not *too* comfortable. Her nerves continued to dance uneasily whenever he was close. But a certain sense of safeness seemed to envelope her. She shrugged off the feeling, blaming it on her being awake too early in the morning.

Michael returned for the glass pot and poured more coffee into her cup, then refilled his own.

"You're welcome to use the downstairs bathroom if you want to clean up," she offered. "I'm going to change."

"Fine. But first I think I'll watch *Sesame Street*. Big Bird's my favorite. I'll go see if Glen wants company."

He eased his large frame away from the counter and, taking his coffee cup with him, left the room. Allie took the stairs quickly and quietly. She was suddenly more anxious than ever to get into some decent clothes.

She tried to hurry, but the hot water felt so wonderful sliding over her sweaty body she could only prolong the sensation. She washed her hair, taking some extra moments to lather in conditioner.

Dressed in white shorts and a casual blue cotton blouse, her damp hair braided neatly at her nape, she looked cool and ready to start the day. Maybe she would make pancakes. Normally Allie hated making breakfast, but somehow this day was different. She noted the empty beds upstairs, realized that Sherry and Dan were up and thought wryly that there should be quite a crowd around the TV set by now.

But when she came downstairs to the kitchen, she was surprised. The small army of helpers that bustled around the kitchen looked familiar, something like her children, but she wouldn't bet on it.

What had he done, she wondered, looking at their leader. A dish towel tied around the old jogging shorts, Michael held a spatula in his hand, which he waved calmly in the air, as a policeman would direct traffic. Country and Western music blasted from the radio. The smell of frying bacon was unmistakable, and Allie's mouth watered. Dan was busy setting the table in the living room, and Sherry importantly carried the paper napkins to him. Allie was sure, though, that she hadn't forgotten there was a man in the kitchen to show off for. Glen stood on a chair at the counter, busily cracking eggs. It was a favorite thing for him to do, and Allie was sure he had lost no time telling Michael all about his new skill. They all looked so busy and happy.

Michael turned to smile at her. "We missed you. I hope you don't mind," he offered almost apologetically, "but I thought I'd get breakfast ready."

"I told him you never cook breakfast, Mom," offered Dan.

"Gee, thanks," she replied wryly, as Michael handed her a fresh cup of coffee. She realized she had left her cup on the upstairs bathroom counter. Before she could react, he encircled her shoulder with one brawny arm and led her to a kitchen chair. The unfamiliar contact stunned her, and it took all the steadiness she could summon to prevent the coffee from spilling onto her hand. "Wait a—"

"I have enough help as it is," he said. "You can watch, though, if you want."

"Okay," she said cheerfully, sitting down at the kitchen table. "It's a real novelty to see someone else at the stove."

"Suit yourself. How do you like your eggs?"

"I don't, usually."

He looked disappointed. "You mean you're not going to try one of my specialties?"

"Which is?" she prompted, sure he had plenty of specialties, with flirting right up there at the top of the list.

"Omelets."

"Okay, I'll give it a try." It was the least she could do. After all, he was cooking breakfast.

"Great." He searched through the drawer and pulled out a whisk. She watched him, something she seemed to have been doing a lot in the past fourteen hours. Sipping the hot coffee and feeling herself come alive now that she was finally awake, she eased into a feeling that was akin to being on vacation.

The quietest helper finished cracking eggs and turned to grin at his mother. The two setting the table were arguing over the proper silverware dispersement. Allie thought of all the sewing she had to do to fill next week's orders and wondered if Michael would want to shop for bicycles today.

"Hey, you two, quit fighting and pour the juice," called Michael.

The fighting dulled to gentle bickering while Dan obediently followed directions. Sherry clung to Michael's leg, kissing his knees and letting the hair on his legs tickle her face.

"Sherry, for heaven's sake!" Allie was embarrassed. Sherry was just too friendly and could make a pest of herself easily. "Come give me a good-morning hug," she said, hoping that would distract the child. Michael looked as if he knew what he was doing at the stove, like the self-sufficient bachelor she assumed he was. "Should I take you to town this morning to look for a bicycle?"

He kept his back to her while he sprinkled cheese on the puffy egg mixture in the skillet. The timing was crucial, and he didn't want to screw it up after bragging about what great omelets he made. "I'd rather wait to hear if I can get a bike shipped from Portland. It'll be easier that way."

"Why? Is that where you're from?" What could be easier than buying something in town today? And how long, she wondered, would it take for him to hear from Portland? Sherry scooted off Allie's lap and ran into the living room to tease Dan again.

"Didn't I tell you that?" He shook the pan, glancing over his shoulder to where she sat. She shook her head. "I'm a silent partner in a sporting goods shop there, so it will be easier—and cheaper—to replace the bike through the store."

"Oh, okay." The cheaper part definitely appealed to her. "How long will that take, do you think?" How long before she had her house and her privacy back?

"Depends. Jake's going to call me back today or tomorrow. Okay, everybody," he called, "we're ready to eat!"

Allie rose slowly and went into the living room where the pastel crepe paper still hung from the ceiling over the table. It gave the house a festive feeling. Maybe she'd leave it up for a few more days. The kids laughed when Michael pretended he was a waiter and served them small sections of the omelet.

"Oops," he said, bending over her shoulder, "I almost forgot the lady of the house." His warm breath tickled her cheek as he plopped a portion of the fluffy eggs onto her plate. "Is this going to be enough?"

"Yes, and it smells wonderful. Thank you," she gulped, remembering her manners as he moved away to the other side of the table. This wasn't fair. She picked up her fork, reminded the children to put their napkins in their laps, and stabbed the eggs. She couldn't look across the table at the man who sat there so cheerfully. Despite her better judgment, she was attracted to him, and had been since she'd seen him in the post office. And it just wasn't fair. He was a stranger, here for as long as it took to replace his bike, that was all. And when he was ready, he'd leave, with nothing more than a casual wave goodbye, just as Paul had. She'd learned a good lesson years ago. And she'd be crazy to risk going through that kind of disappointment again.

WHEN ALLIE ANSWERED the phone Sunday morning she wasn't surprised to hear Barbara's voice. "You're a day late," Allie commented dryly.

"I spent yesterday in Spokane shopping for school clothes with Tina, or I would have been over to meet your houseguest. Tina hasn't stopped babbling about him since Friday night."

"He's not my houseguest. He sleeps in a tent outside," Allie corrected. "And I'd really like him to go somewhere else, but Lydia won't have a cabin free until the end of September."

"What on earth for?" Barbara's voice was incredulous. "I heard he was handsome."

"Well, yes," Allie replied, thinking of Michael's broad shoulders, strong legs, ready smile.

"Is he nice?"

"He cooks breakfast, and seems to like the kids, if that's what you mean."

There was silence on the other end of the phone.

"Barbara? Are you there?"

Her friend's voice returned. "Sorry. I was reaching for an ashtray. This is definitely becoming a cigarette conversation."

"Maybe I should take up smoking then."

"Don't you dare. At the moment you don't have any vices—you're just crazy."

Allie leaned against the counter and peered out the window. The orange tent looked outrageously cozy nestled under the trees. "Just because I don't want company one week before the craft show—"

"There has to be more to it than that," she interrupted. "Why wouldn't you be happy with a handsome man falling into your life? He likes kids, cooks breakfast and sounds like a hunk. Why don't you just keep him? Smash every new bike he buys until he gets the message and stays." Laughter pealed through the receiver.

"You're nuts."

"Just practical. When was the last time you went out on a date?"

"I'm not telling," she replied, unable to remember, but not wanting to admit it. "And besides, just because you're happily married doesn't mean—"

"Doesn't mean," finished Barbara, "that I can't look out for your best interests. There isn't a decent man within thirty miles of your house. The nice ones are married, and the single ones spend their time and money in the bars or else they're up in the mountains shooting animals. It's about time you had some fun."

The lecture didn't faze Allie. "Aren't you out of breath?"

"Where is he now?"

She knew whom Barbara was talking about. "Dan said he jogged to the store to get the Sunday paper."

"Bring him to the picnic. He and Ron can get acquainted. If we think he's dangerous we'll warn you!"

They laughed together. "Jeanne already invited him so I don't have much choice. What time?"

"Two. No, make it three. I have tons of weeding to do."

The screen door banged open. Michael was back. "Sounds fine. See you then." She hung up the phone and turned to say good morning. She hadn't seen him since yesterday afternoon. She'd spent most of the day sewing, trying to finish another quilt for the show. When Michael wasn't around at dinnertime she'd assumed he'd walked down the hill to one of the lakeside restaurants. She'd left the door unlocked at night so he could use the bathroom, but she hadn't heard him come inside the house.

His broad back was to her as he leaned over the narrow kitchen table and dismantled the neat bundle of newspaper. She was sick to death of that green T-shirt. "Good morning," she called.

He turned to smile at her. "Glad you're awake. I brought you something."

"The funnies?" Allie stepped closer to see what was on the table.

He handed her a box of powdered sugar doughnuts, then walked to the cupboard for a coffee cup as if he'd lived in her house for years. He reached past her for the coffeepot, filling the brown mug slowly. "It's Sunday. No Jane Fonda, remember? Don't let me stop you from crawling back into bed, if you want."

"Uh, thanks." She was flabbergasted that he had remembered her casual comment. "But I don't think so." She noticed his dark eyes studying her with interest over the rim of the brown-glazed mug as he lifted it to his lips.

"Would you like to do some laundry today?"

His eyebrows rose at the change in the conversation, but after he swallowed his coffee he nodded. "Are you tired of this shirt, too?"

Allie nodded, "I don't want to hurt your feelings, but..." She hesitated, with a smile. "The washer and dryer are in the sewing room. Feel free."

"Thanks. Where are the kids? It's awfully quiet around here."

"They're upstairs cleaning their bedrooms. It's a Sunday morning tradition."

"Well," he said, smiling, "I think I'll start my own Sunday morning tradition and take the paper and my coffee out onto the deck."

"Want a doughnut, too?" She held out the box she had just opened, wondering if she should join him on the deck. "This was awfully nice of you."

He reached for one. "I'm a nice guy. Haven't you figured that out yet?"

She laughed up into his twinkling eyes. "Nope. But I'll work on it."

"Good. I'll be out on the deck if you need me."

If you need me. The casual words assailed Allie as Michael picked up the newspaper and walked out the door. Why on earth would he think she'd *need* him for anything? *I need you to hit the road*, she wanted to yell after him. *I need my privacy back. I need*—Allie's thoughts stopped, her mind went blank. And suddenly Alice Leonard wasn't sure what she needed at all.

She looked down at the box of doughnuts she still held. Pure heaven. *Go ahead*, a wicked little voice urged, *live a little*.

After eating three of them, she called up the stairs, "Hey, kids, come see what Michael brought!"

THE RIDE TO THE CAMPGROUND was a crowded one, with all of them squeezed into the front seat of the little truck. Sherry sat on Michael's lap, and Glen sat on top of Dan. Allie was glad when they left the paved peninsula road and drove onto the rough gravel of the Forest Service access. The lake was in sight through the scattered pine trees. The small parking lot of the picnic area was packed, but Allie managed to squeeze the truck into a spot under a tree.

"Everyone has to carry something," Allie said as the children hurried to open the door. The truck bed was filled with inflatable rings, air mattresses and food. She handed the eager children their swimming gear and they ran off to find their friends.

"Don't go in the water till I get down there!"

"Okay!" Dan called over his shoulder.

"Let me get this for you," offered Michael, reaching past her and lifting the cooler easily over the tailgate.

Allie grabbed a paper bag full of potato chips and marshmallows. "I hope you like junk food."

"That's what picnics are all about," he replied comfortably as he followed her down the path to the beach. Allie looked around for Jeanne, who usually came early to reserve a group of picnic tables. She found her overseeing three shaded tables grouped around two barbecue stands, where Barbara stood with a sack of charcoal.

"Hi, everybody." Allie set the bag down on a table, and made room for the cooler Michael carried.

"Michael, I'm glad you could come today," Jeanne said with a welcoming smile.

"Well, so am I. It's nice to see you again." He held out his hand to Barbara. "We haven't met. I'm Michael Rhodes."

She quickly wiped the charcoal dust off her hand and shook his. "Barbara Miller. I heard about your bike. That's a shame."

Allie didn't think Barbara looked sorry at all. In fact, Barbara looked quite pleased with the whole situation. "Let's not keep reminding him," said Allie, opening the cooler. "Who wants a cold drink?"

"You wouldn't have any beer in there, would you?"

"Here, Michael, Ron brought some. And so did Bob. Help yourself," offered Barbara, pointing to a green metal cooler by the barbecue. "Hey, Ron!"

They turned to see a sturdy blond man herding two young boys toward the lake.

"Where's Tina?" asked Allie.

Ron pointed toward the beach. "She's watching the other kids." Ron shook hands with Michael as Allie introduced them. In a few minutes the two men opened cold cans of beer and strolled along the sand to the waterfront, where they sat on a sun-bleached log and watched the children play in the lake.

Allie watched Michael adjust Sherry's life jacket before she happily tumbled into the shallow water.

"It's good to see a man around you." Jeanne's soft voice was serious. "And such a nice one, too."

"He'll be gone in a few days, as soon as he gets a new bike shipped from Portland," Allie reminded her. "And I'm not the one-night-stand type."

"So? Ask him to stay longer. He seems happy enough." Barbara gestured toward the beach, where Ron and Michael were deep in conversation.

"A little *too* happy. C'mon," she said, changing the uncomfortable subject, "let's go swimming."

Allie pulled off her shirt and shorts, revealing a rose one-piece bathing suit, and joined the children in the water. While Dan and the other children were trying to balance themselves on a floating log, Sherry and Glen bounced toward their mother, mischievous grins on their glowing faces.

"Hey! Quit splashing!" she protested, laughing.

Glen's grin widened as he paddled around her. "But Mom, you're not wet yet!"

"Give me a minute," she begged. The tank suit flattered her slim figure and firm breasts. All the exercising paid off, she thought, when she caught Michael's appreciative look before he dived into the water beside her.

She took a deep breath and threw herself backward, bracing herself against the shock of the cool water hitting her skin. The children screamed in delight as she turned to pinch their bottoms under the water. She came up for air, water streaming down her face, and brushed the dark strands of hair from her eyes.

"Fair's fair," said Michael, who stood in front of her, his hands on his hips. There was no green T-shirt covering the expanse of gorgeous male chest. Allie found herself staring into a thick mat of curling chest hair that made her long to rest her forehead against it and tickle her nose with its furriness. Little drops of water ran in rivulets down his sides until stopped by the elasticized waist of his navy-blue cotton bathing suit.

"Huh?" She forced herself to look up, with one hand shading her eyes against the sun's glare.

"That wasn't *Glen's* bottom you were grabbing just now," he said, grasping her upper arms and heaving her up and sideways to splash under the water.

She came up sputtering. Of course it had been Glen— he'd been swimming past her when she dived into the water. "Liar!"

He grinned. "You'll never know for sure. Race you to the ropes?"

It would test the limits of her small swimming ability, but she couldn't resist a challenge. She thought she could make it to the markers that enclosed the swimming area. "You're on, pal!"

He outdistanced her easily.

"No fair. You're an athlete," she panted, as they hung together on the rope.

"And you're a lousy swimmer," he teased.

"Why do you think the kids wear life jackets?" she returned, smiling easily at the man beside her. She kicked lazily in the water to stay afloat and rested on the rope, watching him watch her. Sunlight bounced off the water and reflected golden highlights in his dark hair.

"This is the most fun I've had in years," he said. He reached out and surprised himself by touching her face gently. He told himself he wouldn't be sane if he wasn't attracted to the lively woman beside him. And that shiny scrap of pink material she was wearing didn't make things any easier. He wanted to run his hands along her body's length and test his palms against her softness. Instead he drew his finger along her cheekbone, tracing a careful pattern to her parted lips. He watched Allie's eyes darken to the color of shaded pine trees before he bent his head toward her and brushed his lips against hers.

He smelled delicious, she thought, a dangerously male combination of sunshine, fresh water and slight remnants of tangy after-shave. The brief kiss was a bolt of heated light that pierced the most intimate parts of her body. She tightened her grip on the rope.

He drew closer once again, his skin slipping sensuously along hers. It was a tantalizing feeling, and Allie closed her eyes to blot out the sun's reflection. She wanted to blot out more than just the sun, like the other swimmers splashing nearby and the little voice inside telling her she was acting like a sexually-deprived stereotype. She opened her eyes and moved away, even though his hands still cradled her face. "Look, I know you're on vacation and you're a very attractive man, but . . ."

"But?" he offered.

"I don't spend my afternoons kissing strangers and I don't know anything about you so if you don't mind let's keep it that way."

"What way?"

He was being deliberately obtuse. "You'll be leaving in a few days," she said, needing to break the dangerous intimacy that encircled them.

He dropped his hand, but stayed close to her. "Maybe," he murmured, not really sure of anything anymore except the startling physical pull between them.

Allie took a deep breath. *"Definitely,"* she countered, an apology in her voice. She daringly touched his shoulder, effectively separating them by more inches.

"Mommy! Watch me!" Sherry's cries forced Allie to look away from the unreadable expression in Michael's eyes. She realized guiltily that she hadn't been paying close enough attention to the children. Another good reason to keep away from this man, she decided.

"I'm watching," she called, as the little orange-life-jacketed body ducked under the water and popped back up again, sputtering with pleasure at her newfound courage.

"Wonderful!" Allie let go of the rope and swam back to shore, keeping an eye on her courageous daughter. Such new bravery could get her into trouble if she wasn't careful. And as Allie touched the safety of the rocky shore, her fingertips still warm from the smooth heat of Michael's shoulder, she silently repeated the same words to herself.

4

THE PICNIC was a typical hodgepodge of kids, hot dogs, briquettes that stubbornly wouldn't light and the mad passing of food, which almost everyone ate standing up. Michael was relaxed and chatted easily with the other men. Grace and Fred Farmin, who owned a nearby marina, joined them just in time for dinner.

After the introductions were made, Fred and Michael wandered over to the fireplace to put on some more hot dogs and talk fishing. Grace stayed beside Allie. "So that's the mysterious plumber from Friday night. I heard you ran into him the other day."

"In a manner of speaking," she countered dryly. "Now he's camped in my yard. I'm sure the whole neighborhood is wondering what I'm up to. Would you pass the catsup?"

Grace reached over the children's heads and grabbed the bottle. "Here. If you want to be 'up to' anything, just drop the kids off at my house," she offered with a wink.

"You're not supposed to think that way, Grace. You're the older generation."

Grace snorted. "I'm not too old to appreciate a gorgeous hunk of man like your Michael there. And you're not getting any younger yourself."

Allie grinned, then bit into her hot dog. "Why do I get the feeling everyone wants to see me rolling around in the sack with this guy? You all have dirty minds," she teased.

She moved to the end of the table and reached for a spoonful of potato salad.

"Don't talk with your mouth full, dear." Grace smiled wickedly. "I may be gray, but I'm not blind." She gestured toward the other picnic table, where Michael had moved to spoon Jell-O onto Glen and Dan's plates. Sherry stood beside him, holding on to his shirt. "You—all four of you—could use a man in your lives," she continued, her voice serious and thoughtful.

"Not him, not now." Allie stabbed her fork into her salad, surprised that her hand was trembling.

"Hey, Grace! Come and get it!" Fred waved a long-handled fork in their direction.

"Stick it in a bun, I'm coming," she returned. She whispered to Allie, "Take some advice from an old lady, honey. And don't let the past—whatever it was your husband did—tie you up in knots for the rest of your life."

Allie could only stare as Grace walked away. Since she'd moved here she had avoided talking about the past. Was she that transparent? None of her friends had known Paul, and she'd never talked much about the life she'd had before moving to Hope. No one knew why her husband had left her or of the tragic way Sherry had become part of the family. Allie had carefully constructed an emotional shelter for herself and the children so they would never be hurt again. She liked her life just the way it was. She watched the happy chaos of friends and children and suddenly felt uncertain.

Michael looked up and his warm brown eyes smiled into hers. He pointed to an empty place on the bench in front of him. Allie hesitated, then strode toward him. She'd just have to make the best of it.

"WOULD YOU like some wine?"

Allie glanced away from the pink-and-gold sunset that framed the mountains over the lake—a picture postcard scene she tried never to take for granted. Michael stood there, offering a plastic cup.

She reached for it, her fingers brushing his for a brief electric second until he slowly released it to her. "Thanks." She moved toward the middle of the log, a silent but reluctant invitation for him to join her in front of the camp fire pit.

Michael noticed her hesitation and realized he shouldn't have intruded upon her privacy. He sat down close to her anyway. "Hiding?"

"Just enjoying the peace and quiet, I guess." The water made little lapping sounds onto the rocky beach.

"I can see what you mean," he agreed, looking toward the group of children who were using the last bit of sunlight to finish a giant sand castle on the far end of the beach. For some reason they had selected a pile of sand directly underneath the unused volleyball net.

Allie sipped at the cool white wine, grateful for something to do. Michael's warm bulk beside her was oddly arousing, and his presence protected her from the chilling breeze that had slipped down from the mountain.

"We were interrupted this afternoon," he began, casually enfolding her free hand with his own.

She didn't pretend to misunderstand. "Which was probably a good thing." She left her hand in his, although she would have liked to tug it away.

"We were interrupted," he repeated as if he hadn't heard her words, "before I could explain why I kissed you."

"Look, Michael—" her face flushed with embarrassment "—I'm not any better at this than I am at swimming," she admitted. "You don't have to explain anything. We can just forget about it, okay?"

"I make you uncomfortable."

"Well, of course you do."

"Why?"

Didn't the man realize the way women reacted to him? "Well, for one thing, I'm worried I'm going to have to spend the next few days being chased around my house by an oversexed athlete." She'd never been a live-for-the-moment kind of person, and she wasn't about to start now.

He chuckled. "You're a very tempting lady. I've never heard myself described that way." And he hoped no one he knew would ever hear it, either, especially his teenage football team. Now there was a group of oversexed athletes. Somehow, he knew, he had to make her understand. He took the wine from her and set it on the sand behind the log. Cupping her face in his hands, he turned her toward him. He wanted to explore what he felt, he wanted to continue on the path he'd wandered onto, away from his destination and the parts of his life that had brought him only pain. "You feel it, too," he murmured, "you can't deny that." He tasted the softness of her lower lip, feeling the quiver there that betrayed her, tempting him to deepen a kiss he'd only meant to be brief.

Allie knew she should pull away, but he was right. She liked what she was feeling and it was hard to resist the building heat between them. She pressed her palms onto her thighs to keep herself from pulling him closer.

He felt her stiffen and ended the kiss, frowning when he saw her rub her hands on her legs. "You're cold."

I'm crazy, she thought, peering past him to see if anyone was watching, but she and Michael were hidden in the shadows of the pines.

They sat together in silence for a moment, as the setting sun hung above the mountaintops.

"I've been instructed to build a camp fire." He slipped off the log to kick some driftwood into the pit. "I'm not sure why I was assigned this job," he said easily, "but Barbara gave me matches and part of a paper bag."

"Because you look like an outdoorsman." His tan came from long hours outside, and he didn't have the body of someone who worked behind a desk all day. Maybe he went to one of those weight lifting places. But the hands that had caressed her face a moment ago had been rough. And strong.

"Appearances are deceiving. I don't even know how to work that stove I told Dan about. I'll have to get busy and read the directions before he remembers my promise."

"Oh, he'll remember, all right." She watched as he arranged the wood around the paper, which quickly caught fire, burning the dry wood easily. The man could do nothing wrong.

Michael took his place on the log and relaxed, legs outstretched so his large untied tennis shoes were closer to the fire.

They watched as the other couples meandered down the beach toward the fire. Jeanne was dangling a bag of marshmallows in front of the busy children.

"We're about to roast marshmallows, all of us," Allie said.

"I haven't done that in years." The thread of pleasure in his warm voice made Allie turn to him curiously.

"Why not?"

"I guess it's something I just forgot about."

"Well, here's your chance. The hordes are descending. Looks like Barbara has collected sticks. She's very organized about all of this."

"Mom! Do you have a stick?" cried Glen, in a cloud of sandy dust. His face was smeared with dirt, his voice excited. The firelight flickered in the breeze. Ashes swung toward them, the smoke making Allie cough.

"Here, Glen," called Barbara. "I collected enough for everyone." She handed out sticks. "Now all we have to do is make sure they don't burn each other in the process."

"Where are the others?"

"Coming. They went back for wine and coffee."

The children surrounded the camp fire, passing the marshmallow bag back and forth.

Sherry leaned against Michael, holding out a marshmallow to him. "Want one?"

"Sure," he said, popping it into his mouth.

She frowned up at him. "You're s'posed to cook it first," she scolded.

"Okay. Let's cook the next one. Will you help me?"

"'Kay," she agreed happily, holding out the stick to him and cuddling closer.

"This kid's a real charmer, Allie," he murmured, as he speared a marshmallow onto the stick. "Are you sure she's only three?"

"I think she was *born* old," she replied, enjoying the cozy scene beside her. It gave her a strange pang, seeing Sherry like that. The child had never known a father's love and attention. What she got was secondhand from the other fathers, who were generous with their time with all the children, but for Sherry—and yes, for herself, too, she admitted—it wasn't enough. And it was definitely not the same as having the real thing.

Glen and Danny inched closer. Dan handed a toasted offering to his mother.

"You eat the first one, honey," she declined.

"It's okay, Mom, there's plenty and I'll make doubles next."

She took the gooey candy from the stick and popped it into her mouth. It was sweet and sticky and hot, and the taste was absolutely delicious. "Mmm . . . thanks."

"You two want sticks?" asked Barbara from the other side of the pit.

Michael answered for them, as if he was part of the couple they so accidentally made. "We have our hands full now." He speared two marshmallows onto Glen's stick and helped him hold it over the coals, showing the small boy where to position it so it wouldn't burn.

"But I like 'em black," Glen protested.

Michael laughed, looking at Allie before turning back to the child. "Then go for it—jam it right into the flames. Just don't burn yourself."

Allie watched them. Michael's face was darker in the firelight; mysterious shadows highlighted the handsome planes of his face.

The rosy glow of the sunset topped the distant mountains before disappearing quickly into a flush of darkness. Soon everyone had gathered by the fire, Grace sitting on the other side of Allie. The adults chatted quietly, keeping a careful eye on the rambunctious children. Jeanne and Bob held hands, standing by the fire. Jeanne tossed another bag of marshmallows at Michael. "Here," she said, "you're in charge."

"Fine," he agreed with a pleasant smile. "Do you have picnics like this often?"

"Sure. Don't you have picnics in Oregon? Isn't that where Bob said you were from?"

"Portland. And I haven't had much time in the past years for just pure fun."

"Well, why not?" Barbara piped up, never shy about asking questions. Allie, too, waited to hear what he would say.

"I teach high school and coach football."

"But you have summers off," Allie interjected. A teacher. That explained his patience with the children.

"Not until this year. A friend and I started a sports shop a few years ago, which turned out to take more time than I ever suspected it would. But this year I had to . . ." He hesitated. "I needed some time away, so I'm taking the first semester as a leave of absence."

"Will you go back to teaching?" Allie surprised herself by asking. Why should she want to know any more about this man? Better he stay a stranger.

"I don't know," he said quietly. And he meant it, he realized. He didn't know what path his life would take once the summer was over. Once he had learned what had happened to his daughter and confronted the place where she'd died. He'd let the pleasantness of the day lull him into forgetting why he'd made this trip.

The sizzling of the fire was the only sound to break the silence. A lone fisherman cut his boat's engine and drifted neatly beside a nearby dock. The children were quiet, concentrating on their roasting marshmallows. Even Barbara had nothing to say, as reluctant as Allie to intrude any further into Michael's personal thoughts.

"I brought a thermos of coffee. Any takers?" Grace held up a stack of Styrofoam cups.

Allie stood, holding her empty cup. "None for me, thanks. I'd better go gather our things together while there's still a little light."

"I'll help you," Michael offered.

"Stay. Please. Keep Sherry from falling into the fire while I'm gone."

"All right. Here, babe," he said to the child, "have another marshmallow."

"Tank you berry much."

"You're berry welcome," he replied, his deep voice exploding into a chuckle.

Allie walked away quickly, kicking up little clouds of sand in her haste. The piny picnic area offered solitude. She had to get away, away from the cozy intimacy of the fire, the coffee, the wine and the evening that had settled so closely around them. What was happening to her? Everything else had seemed to fade into the background while she had contemplated his voice, his words, wondering who he was . . .

Allie grabbed her soggy towels and the ice chest, dropping a bag of garbage into a can on the way to the truck. Always the responsible citizen, she thought wryly. She hesitated to return to the others, afraid to test the strength of the spell woven around the camp fire. She was saved the trouble, for out of the darkness came Michael carrying a sleeping child. The boys followed behind, lugging their air mattresses.

Michael's low voice carried through the darkness. "She's asleep. I didn't notice until her last marshmallow burned up."

"Thanks. I think I've got everything in the truck."

He followed her back to the parking area. "I said good-night to everyone for you."

"Oh, good," she said, anxious to put the children in bed. They jumbled together in the front seat of the truck, with Glen squeezed into a tiny space behind the seat. It was a quiet ride home. Allie drove the truck with her usual competence along the winding gravel road that led out of the campground. They passed many camp fires, their glow illuminating the trailers and tents of the people fortunate enough to have found a campsite. The ride home in the quiet darkness went quickly, and soon Allie parked the truck in the driveway. She left the lights on so her passengers could make their way down the steps.

"C'mon, Glen, hop out and go right into the bathroom and wash up." She eyed the sticky mess on his face as he wiggled over her lap and out the truck door. "Dan, here are the keys. Unlock the door, then get your pajamas on."

"Can I sleep in my underwear?" he asked hopefully.

"No."

She got out of the truck and helped Dan hop down. Michael shielded Sherry's closed eyes from the overhead glow of the dome light. "Any instructions for me, Sarge?"

Allie smiled ruefully. "Sorry. I know I sound like a drill sergeant sometimes."

"No. Just a mother." He looked tenderly at the child in his arms. "I'll carry her down if you'll open the door for me."

She walked around to his side of the truck. "Thanks," she whispered as she unlatched the door and helped him ease himself and Sherry off the seat. But when she saw his face in the light before he stepped away into the darkness she caught a look that prevented her from saying anything else to him. That look could only be pain. She stared as he passed her, his eyes dark, his mouth set in a straight line, tension in his jaw that belied the gentle cradling of her daughter in his arms. What on earth was wrong? She waited as he went down to the house. After she heard the screen door slam shut she turned off the headlights and shut the door of the truck before making her way down the steps.

Don't even think about it, she warned herself as she stepped into the kitchen. It was too easy for her to take on another person's problems. Somehow their pain snaked around and caught her up, too. She'd never been able to ignore someone who was suffering, turning herself into a one-woman sympathy factory. "Not this time," she muttered, kicking off her sandals. This time she would pretend she hadn't glimpsed a thing and just put it out of her mind. If she started to feel sorry for him she'd be a goner.

Michael came down the stairs, walking heavily. He didn't try to disguise how upset he was, but avoided her eyes. "I tucked her in just the way she was."

"Thanks again. Michael, is there anything—" *Don't ask for the story of his life, just say good-night.* "Well, good night."

"See you in the morning." He left quickly, closing the door quietly behind him.

5

IT WAS GOING TO BE one of those Monday mornings. Allie groaned as the phone rang insistently once again. She hadn't had three spare minutes since she got out of the shower. She looked at her watch. Was it only nine o'clock?

Putting the quilt back on the table, she raced Sherry to the phone.

"Hello?" She unwrapped her daughter's grasping fingers from the telephone cord and shooed her back to her breakfast.

"Hello." The man's voice sounded very far away. He hesitated for a moment. "I have a message for Michael Rhodes. Is this where he can be reached?"

"One moment, please. I'll check," Allie said, unconsciously imitating the formal speech of the caller. She looked out the kitchen window at the tent. The orange monstrosity was still zipped shut.

She sighed, set the phone down on the counter and stepped outside to the deck.

"Michael!" she called, hesitating to get any closer. Visions of a bear in his cave ran through her mind as she tiptoed onto the grass, closer to the tent.

"Hey, Michael!" she tried again. Maybe he was off jogging. And how the heck was she supposed to knock on a tent?

She poked at it irritably with her foot, connecting with something solid.

"Ow, hmph?"

"You have a phone call."

"Okay, I'm coming." His deep voice was muffled.

Allie heard the rustle of his large body brushing the nylon walls. The sound of a zipper made her scurry back onto the deck. She hadn't remembered what an intimate sound that was. What had possessed her to hang around outside his tent? She popped back through the open door and into the living room, glad to see Sherry curled up on the couch watching *Mr. Rogers* and not chattering into the telephone receiver.

She picked up the phone. "He's coming."

"Oh, good. I thought we might have been cut off."

"No, it just took me a minute to locate Mr. Rhodes," she answered formally once again, hoping the slight sarcasm didn't come through to the caller.

Michael entered through the kitchen door, yawning and running his hand through his unruly hair. He wore jeans and an unbuttoned shirt, his bare feet padded silently across the floor. She handed him the receiver and returned to the living room.

She heard him greet the caller, but didn't catch his name. She eavesdropped shamelessly. After all, this was her house, wasn't it? She moved the pincushion to the center of the table. And she was a very busy person trying to get some work done.

"Great," he said. "When?"

There was silence as the caller answered his question. Allie wondered if that had something to do with getting a replacement for the mangled bike stashed in her garage. She had called her insurance company this morning. They had said they'd try to cut through the red tape and hurry things along, but it could be more than a week before she would know anything.

"Thanks. Any word from Wentworth?"

Who was Wentworth? Allie pinned the rose border onto the quilt block and surveyed it critically. Pillows were not her favorite thing to make but they tended to sell well so she usually had a selection handy. The pinwheel design was pretty, its corners meeting precisely. Satisfied, she took the block to the sewing machine and proceeded to carefully stitch the fabric. The noise of the machine kept her from hearing the rest of Michael's conversation.

"Hi, there," Michael said from the doorway. He walked closer and pulled a chair up to the fabric-laden table and studied the woman so intent upon guiding pink material through the sewing machine. To his horror, she had pins stuck between her pressed lips. "Don't talk," he begged.

Allie lifted her foot from the pedal and removed the pins from her mouth. He handed her the pincushion and she stabbed the pins into its plump surface. "What do you want?" She sighed when she realized how crabby she sounded.

"Get up on the wrong side of the bed this morning?" he teased.

"At least I got up," she said pointedly, then winced. "Don't mind me. I'm usually crabby right before a show. I panic thinking I haven't made enough." She smiled wryly at him over the piles of fabric covering the table. "Don't take it too personally."

"That was my partner on the phone saying he can ship me a bike within the week. It'll probably take three or four days to get there, so you'll have to put up with me for a little while longer." He found himself looking forward to the extra days in this home.

Michael leaned forward, his shirt gaping in front of him. Allie wished he'd button it. That hairy brown chest was destroying all her concentration for rose-flowered pinwheel pillow tops.

"Sure," she said slowly, looking back at the fabric she held pressed under the machine's needle. "I guess we can manage. Uh, how much is this new bike going to cost?"

"Let's not worry about that until it gets here."

That wasn't the answer she wanted to hear. "I talked to my insurance company today. There'll be forms to fill out and I'd like to know where I stand—"

"Is that what *this*—" he pointed to the mounds of sewing "—is all about?"

"This?" she echoed. He was frowning again.

"Are you sewing to pay for my bike?"

"Well, it'll probably work out that way. Yes."

"Good Lord! That's ridiculous."

"No, it's not. I sew all the time." She stared at him, her green eyes wide. He was good looking—even handsome—at his calm, self-controlled best. But scrape the restraint off the surface and get him riled up, and he was magnificent. She didn't have any desire to answer him, preferring to watch a little longer and see what happened next.

He stood up. For a moment she thought he was going to turn around and walk out, but he stepped closer and leaned over her, bracing himself with his hand on the back of her chair. "If you think I'm the kind of man who will let you work yourself sick doing some kind of 'Waltons' imitation to pay for a stupid luxury—"

"I loved that show," she whispered, knowing if she leaned forward just a few inches she could rub her cheek against the sandpaper of his unshaved jaw. A jaw clenched in anger. What on earth was he upset about?

"—like a bicycle," he continued as if he hadn't heard her, his dark eyes snapping angrily, "then you are an idiot."

"Hey, now wait just a minute!" He couldn't call her names.

"Save your pennies," he ordered. He straightened to his full height and looked down at her. "I'll need your truck for a few hours."

Pennies? He didn't have any idea how expensive her quilts were or the enthusiastic reviews she'd received at an exclusive Spokane boutique last Christmas. She raised an eyebrow, questioning his demanding tone. "Why?"

"Errands."

She bent over her sewing, feigning unconcern. "The keys are hanging on a hook by the back door. And you can drive straight to hell and back, for all I care." She pushed down on the pedal, the machine whirring into action as she fed the material through it. If he had anything else to say she didn't hear it.

The rest of the day passed quietly. The boys returned from a friend's house at lunchtime and, sensing their mother's preoccupation with the sewing machine, were content to spend the cloudy afternoon in their playhouse. Sherry soon tired of making necklaces from long scraps of calico, and went uncomplaining upstairs for her nap.

By the time Allie was ready to think about making dinner there were a dozen pillow tops ready to be stuffed with polyester filling. She switched off the machine with a grateful sigh, and pushed the chair away from the table. Her back muscles were tight as she stretched her arms over her head. It had been a productive afternoon, as quiet as the morning had been hectic. But her argument with Michael was still on her mind. She hadn't liked feeling crabby or telling someone to go to hell, but he had called her an idiot and she'd spoken without thinking. Somehow she'd have to smooth it over.

"Michael's back!" Danny called. His excited voice carried through the open window. "Hey, Michael! Come see the playhouse! I made a ramp!"

Allie heard the answering rumble of his voice as the kitchen door opened. Small feet thundered after him.

"Oh, boy, what kind?" piped Glen.

What kind of what? Allie wondered. She strolled into the kitchen, relieved to have Michael back safely. It had been a little worrisome to let a stranger drive off with her only means of transportation.

He looked pleased with himself as he put two flat white boxes on the counter. He didn't seem angry anymore, she noted. His shirt was buttoned and neatly tucked into his jeans. He must have found time to shave, she realized, because he had that squeaky-clean athlete-television-commercial appearance again.

"Dinner. Do you mind?" He looked at her for the first time since he'd walked in, a self-satisfied gleam in those dark eyes of his. She wondered what he'd been doing all day.

"I'd have to be an ⸱ to mind someone bringing dinner." She smiled to show she was just teasing. "It was thoughtful of you, thanks." She turned to the boys who danced excitedly around Michael. "You guys go wash up, then go upstairs and wake Sherry—*nicely*. Don't tell her it's Christmas morning like you did the last time."

They giggled and ran upstairs.

"I lost my temper this morning." There was a strong undercurrent of apology in his voice and Allie sensed he didn't apologize easily.

"Me, too."

He smiled down at her. "Friends?"

"On one condition," she agreed, going to the counter and lifting the lid of the top box. "That there's pepperoni in here." The pizza was dotted heavily with the spicy sausage.

"I'm safe, then?"

"I'm your friend for life." She turned back to grin at him, her dancing green eyes laughed up into his, lightening his thoughtful expression. For a second she caught her breath at the feeling of relief that swept through her body. Relief, bologna, she thought. This is pure unadulterated longing.

If she only knew what those green eyes of hers did to him, Michael mused. Nothing to do with being friends, that was certain. He tried to concentrate on food. "You have to bake them."

She watched his lips move, heard the husky tones of his voice, but could not focus on his words. She wished he'd kiss her again, the way he had last night on the beach. She prayed he wouldn't. "What?"

"They're not cooked."

"Oh." She quit staring at him and moved over to turn on the oven. *Stop acting like an infatuated teenager and just feed your family,* she told herself. But she was aware of him, right down to her bare toes, as he walked behind her to peer into the living room.

"Finished yet?"

"With pillows, yes. Your timing is terrific. I was just trying to figure out what to have for dinner."

He cleared his throat. "I'm glad I could help. What do you do with the things you don't sell?"

"There's another big show in Montana, the Huckleberry Festival. I'm signed up for that. The rest will go to a craft co-op in Sandpoint. They take a commission, so I like to sell as much as I can myself." She grabbed a pot holder, opened the oven door and pulled out the top rack.

"Here. I'll do it." He came over and slid the large pizza off its cardboard circle and onto the rack.

"You're good at that." She handed him the pot holder.

"I've had a lot of practice. Living alone makes you an expert on baking take-out pizza." He slid the rack back into the oven and shut the door. Again there was a shadow of pain across his face.

"Have you always? Lived alone, I mean?" There. It was out. She could have bitten off her tongue when he turned away, his dark eyes strangely bleak.

"No. I'm divorced," he murmured, adding, "I'll go get the rest of the groceries," before he walked quickly out of the kitchen to the backyard.

Allie felt terrible for having forced him to reveal something that was obviously still painful. She knew how much it hurt. For a long time after signing the divorce papers she had felt like a failure. The delicate thread of friendship connecting her with Michael this afternoon wasn't strong enough to hold the weight of past mistakes and personal histories. She would have to be more careful to remember that from now on.

IT WAS AFTER TEN O'CLOCK, the children were exhausted in their beds. Bags of polyester stuffing littered the carpet while Allie, still dressed in baggy cotton pants and a T-shirt, curled up on the couch with a stack of pillow tops beside her and a half-eaten package of Oreo cookies on the coffee table nearby. She grabbed another handful of stuffing and shoved it into the side opening of the patchwork pillow, continuing to stuff until she could poke a pencil, eraser-end first, into the corners to make them full and pointed. She worked quickly, without any wasted movements, but her thoughts were of Michael. She didn't understand how he had become so much a part of the family in just a few days. But his presence was something less than comfortable, she decided wryly, remembering her body's involuntary reactions whenever he was near.

It had been such a long evening. When Michael had returned to the kitchen with armloads of groceries Allie had protested. He'd quietly ignored her objections, dangling Oreos and boxes of brand-name cereal in front of the children. He had seemed quite at ease after returning, and Allie had been wise enough to ignore what had happened earlier. She wanted peace and quiet, and that meant no more scenes, however little they might be.

Peace and quiet, she told herself with a sigh as she reached for a cookie. That's certainly what she had right now and, as Glen would say, it was no fun. A movie was on television, but it wasn't as exciting as the *TV Guide* said it would be. The wind made the trees rustle outside so she had trouble hearing what the actors were saying, but it didn't matter.

The breeze whipped through the screen on the sliding glass door, whisking strips of fabric onto the floor. The rustle of the trees became louder, and Allie went to the window to look. She heard shouting down at the marina, and the sound of the waves hitting the docks. Grace and Fred would be working late tonight to secure boats. Somewhere outside a board banged and metal clanked against a building. Allie hurried out onto the deck to rescue her tablecloth.

"Looks like a storm," Michael murmured from the shadows.

Allie jumped, startled. "For heaven's sake!"

"Sorry." He came closer, into the triangle of light from the doorway. He touched her shoulder in a reassuring gesture, but the contact had the opposite effect upon Allie's tense muscles. She felt as if she'd been stung.

Michael continued to explain, "I've been watching the sky, wondering what the weather was going to do."

As if in answer, lightning shot in jagged fingers over the mountains across the lake. Allie shivered and moved away from Michael's touch. Thunder rumbled far in the distance like some ominous warning of danger.

"Beautiful," he said admiringly.

Allie looked over to the man beside her. "Scary," she countered, before gathering up the tablecloth and moving toward the door. She returned to the living room, leaving him outside to watch the lightning. More of it stabbed the sky, and the thunder grew louder as the storm approached.

She went upstairs to close the windows and make sure the children were asleep. Satisfied the coming storm hadn't awakened them, Allie tiptoed downstairs. Michael was just closing the kitchen door. His nylon packs and sleeping bag were piled on the floor.

"Going somewhere?" She had a feeling she wasn't going to like the answer.

"Not far." He smiled, picked up his sleeping bag and slung it over his shoulder. "I don't feel like being electrocuted tonight." He moved past her toward the living room.

"What's that supposed to mean?" She followed him into the cluttered living room and watched as he set his sleeping bag on the carpet.

"It means I'm sleeping inside." He frowned at the piles of pillows and stuffing that littered the couch. "I'll set up when you're through."

Allie understood his longing glance at the couch and forgot about objecting to the sleeping arrangements. Besides, sleeping on the ground couldn't be comfortable. "No problem. I'll sit in the chair. I can stuff these things anywhere." She was glad to have the company, though she wouldn't have admitted it to anyone but herself.

She moved the sewing quickly, releasing the couch to him. He spread his sleeping bag across it like a navy cocoon.

Michael frowned at the television set then quickly unplugged it. "You really shouldn't have this on during a storm," he informed her. "The antenna might attract lightning."

"I know. I forgot." A nervous thread ran through her simple words. She couldn't identify the feeling. Maybe it was all the electricity in the air. Or the barometric pressure. It certainly couldn't have anything to do with the intimacy of Michael's sleeping bag spread nearby, or the man himself pacing in front of the windows. She sat in the chair and busied herself with another pillow.

A huge clap of thunder shook the house. "It's getting closer," he muttered and finally settled on the couch. He could tell Allie didn't like storms. The delicate bones in her fingers were showing white under the smooth tan skin where she gripped the pencil, and she was curled up in that chair as if she was trying to hide. He wanted to hold her, to ease each tense muscle with his hands and his lips. The aching in his gut increased sharply.

She glanced up from her work to see his dark gaze upon her. His words took on new meaning, and her throat was suddenly dry as she answered, "Let's hope it rains."

"Why?"

Why wouldn't he turn away and look out the window again? "The fire danger's high. And if there's no rain with the lightning there can be forest fires."

"Dry lightning," he echoed. "Yes, I've heard of it."

Allie shifted her gaze away from him, unsettled by the conversation and the approaching storm. And the intense way Michael looked at her. She tried to change the subject. "I hope Sherry doesn't wake up. She's terrified of storms."

"I'll go check on her." He stood and left the room, grateful for something to do.

The sudden emptiness surprised Allie. When Michael returned, the room filled with warmth again.

"She's snoring. I don't think she's heard a thing," he assured her. "What about you? You're looking a little white around the edges. You don't like storms, do you?"

She shook her head. "Not one bit. There are too many trees around."

"Do you have anything besides beer in the house?"

She thought for a minute. "There's wine left from the party. And Barbara gave me some Kahlúa for my birthday."

"I'll make some coffee with Kahlúa," he decided. "You're shivering."

And he looked as if he needed something to do besides pace, she observed. "Sounds like a good idea. There's a jar of instant coffee in the spice cupboard and the Kahlúa is in the cabinet above the sink, I hope."

He disappeared into the kitchen, and she could hear him rummaging around. As always, she was amazed how at home he was in her house.

"Do you have a teakettle or should I use a pan?" he called.

"Put hot water in mugs and zap them in the microwave for a few minutes." Minutes later Michael returned, carrying steaming cups. He set them down on the old wooden coffee table after Allie had rearranged the pincushion, scissors and cookies to make room.

She took a tentative sip of her coffee. It felt hot and rich on her tongue. She fought the sudden urge to drink it all in one gulp and fix herself another.

"Mmm," she murmured, "this is wonderful."

"I was a bartender in college."

"This was a good idea," she told him as the lightning flashed and thunder shook the house. She smiled weakly. "I didn't hear anything, did you?"

He shook his head, his face serious in the lamplight. He sat on top of the sleeping bag and leaned back on the couch, his feet bare, long legs clad in well-worn jeans. His white football shirt's orange lettering spelled something she couldn't read from where she sat. He looked comfortable, and totally at ease, but there was something in his expression that made Allie wonder what he was going to say next. Or was her imagination overactive tonight?

She should be stuffing, she told herself. Reluctantly, she put her drink down and picked up another pillow top and an opened bag of fluffy polyester filling.

"I talked with your insurance agency today."

She looked up, surprised. Well, she supposed it was natural he would want to get the information himself. "Did you hurry them along?"

"No, I canceled the claim."

She dropped the pillow from her lap. "Why?"

He put his cup on the table, then slid back on the couch, his arms behind his head. "My store can handle it."

"But you shouldn't have to. It was my fault."

"Forget it." He wished she would, but he figured he'd have an argument on his hands.

"I'm not sewing just to pay for your bike, you know." She remembered the conversation of this morning. "And besides, I make good money—" Lightning crackled close to the house. Allie wondered what Michael would do if she pushed him aside and jumped into his sleeping bag. The storm made her feel as prickly as the pincushion on the coffee table.

"That's not the point."

"Then what is?" she demanded. He looked so sure of himself as he sat there in front of her, as if he was used to getting his way. She fought the urge to fling the now-plump pillow into his broad chest.

"What you do with your profits is no business of mine," he said.

"You don't have to be so stubborn about it. I *like* to sew. I like to create things—beautiful things, I hope—that people will use and enjoy for years. And I just want to pay for what I owe, without charity." She lifted her chin while she talked, as if to show she couldn't be bossed around.

He swore under his breath. "I don't believe it. You're trying to make me lose my temper again." He took a deep breath and studied her carefully. Pride. He should recognize it when faced with it. Suddenly he laughed. "How about if I pay you room and board while I'm here?"

"Don't be ridiculous," she said in an insulted tone of voice. "No way."

"Then we're even," he stated. "I figure a vacation in Hope is worth the price of a new bicycle." He knew he had her with that one and congratulated himself for quick thinking.

She hesitated. "I think I'm being conned."

"Deal?" He reached across the table to offer his hand.

His dark eyes gleamed with satisfaction when she smiled back at him. Allie felt as if she was agreeing to more than she bargained for, but she couldn't refuse his appeal. She leaned forward and grasped his hand. "Deal." The connection they made was strong, the power behind it a shock to them both. Lightning slammed against the earth once more, and Allie unconsciously tightened her grip on Michael's fingers.

The lights went out. The hum of the refrigerator halted with a slow whine. Darkness abruptly filled the room. Allie didn't move, grateful for Michael's solid grasp.

"Don't let go," she whispered.

"Never," he said, his voice a rich velvet promise. "I'll come over to you. Don't move."

"Be careful. The table's in the way."

She heard the rustle of the sleeping bag, then he was close, pulling her up to stand beside him, their hands still clasped.

He cupped her face with his free hand. "Pretty good timing, wouldn't you say?"

The thread of laughter in his voice made her realize she was behaving like an eight-year-old. She had managed to get through storms worse than this one. But maybe it wasn't the weather that made her nerves stand on end. He was teasing her. Thank goodness he didn't realize he was making her knees turn to jelly. When her eyes began to adjust to the dark she could see the outline of his shoulders. "Are you, uh, taking credit for the storm?"

He continued his exploration of her face, one coarse thumb tracing the line of satin cheekbone and down to gently brush across her lips. "No. But I've made you smile."

"You can't see," she murmured against the enticing roughness of his skin. He'd made her smile, all right, while streaks of awareness heated her body.

"I can feel."

She had to stop this. "We need candles."

He outlined the curve of her lips and then reluctantly dropped his hand. "All right. Where do you keep them?"

"In the kitchen drawer, or at least, they used to be there. There's a kerosene lamp high above the stove, beside the turkey roaster." She couldn't resist adding, "The Waltons gave it to me."

"You're not going to let me forget that, are you?" came the amused voice in the darkness.

"Nope."

"Let's find a flashlight first."

"Glen took it. I don't know if he put it back." She knew he hadn't. What kid ever returned a flashlight? "Maybe it's under his bed."

"Never mind. There's one in my pack by the back door." He pulled her with him, tugging the fine-boned hand gently.

"Are we Siamese twins?" She wasn't complaining, but she needed to hear his voice as they stepped carefully through the darkness. Especially since the kitchen was blacker than the living room had been.

"Yes, for now. If I left you alone you'd figure out how to sew something in the dark. I've never met such a busy person."

"I don't believe in being bored." She ran her free hand along the kitchen counter.

"No kidding. Haven't you ever heard of relaxation?"

"Sure. I go to the beach."

"Watching three kids to make sure they don't drown is not my idea of relaxation."

"Could we talk about this another time, like when there's electricity?" She touched the wall. "We must be close."

He let go of her hand and she heard his low chuckle in the darkness. "Stay right here. I'll find my flashlight."

There was the whisper of nylon, then a click as a beam of light shone near the floor. "There."

"Oh, good. Give it to me and I'll find the candles."

He handed it to her and followed as she rummaged through one of the drawers. "I should be used to this, but it catches me by surprise every time it happens. Usually I just go to bed." She stopped talking, glad he couldn't see her face in the darkness. What a thing to say! As if it wasn't awkward enough in here already, she had to go mentioning bed.

"I'd hate to interrupt your routine," he said wryly.

Deciding to ignore that comment, she found some red Christmas candles and two candle holders and set them on the counter. Next were matches, and when she lit the candles the glow was disturbingly intimate.

"You take the flashlight," he said, "and I'll carry the candles into the living room."

He arranged the candles on the coffee table and they sank back into their respective seats.

"Now, where were we?"

She reached for her coffee cup. "Drinking coffee—which isn't hot anymore," she said, sipping a little. "But it still tastes good." She glanced around the dark room. The only lights were in a house far across the lake, where the owner had his own generator.

Another gust of wind rattled the windows, but no more lightning highlighted the mountaintops across the bay. Rain began to pelt against the glass and pounded heavily onto the grass and trees.

Allie grabbed the flashlight. "Uh-oh. I'd better close the windows. I did the ones upstairs already, just in case."

He hurried to close the sliding door. "Anything else?"

"The window over the sink," she said and they both went to it, reaching it at the same time. His arms were longer and he tried to shut it with a strong tug at the wood. It stuck, while the rain blew in and sprinkled his arms.

"Just a minute." Allie hoisted herself onto the counter and perched near the window. Her cotton slacks absorbed little puddles of rainwater as she kneeled over to push. "Now try," she said, and he pulled as she pushed downward. The window finally shut with a thud. She looked over her shoulder at him. "Old house," she explained with a grin as raindrops trickled down her face.

"Come down from there before you slip and break your neck," he grumbled, reaching for her.

It was the most natural thing in the world to lean into his arms, strong arms that reached to hold her, to keep her safe. It was the easiest motion, the warmest feeling. She let herself be pulled against his large solid chest as her toes gently touched the floor.

He kept his arms around her, her slim body tucked neatly against his, the counter edge nudging her waist as if to push her closer to the man holding her in the darkness. Without knowing what came over her, she slipped her arms past his shoulders, resting her fingertips lightly against the warmth and softness of his nape. The flashlight lay forgotten on the counter, shining its useless circle toward the stove, allowing Michael and Allie to remain in privacy.

She braved a look up at his face, admiring the strong jaw outlined in the night, until the warmth of his brown eyes mesmerized her. Until he bent slowly toward her, and kissed her lightly. His lips were warm and soft, and she barely had time to respond before the kiss was over. He touched her face, gently wiping the drops of rain away with the palms of his hands. He leaned still closer to her, although he held her no longer.

She didn't know what she missed more—the feel of him holding her or the sweet sensation of his lips touching hers. Somehow she felt reassured, and the sharp longing that raced through her body startled her with its intensity. He must have felt it, too, because he held her face in his big hands and looked down at her, questioning, waiting, wondering.

She started to smile, the barest touch of expression, as she looked into his eyes once more. What was he thinking? Suddenly she didn't care, she just had to feel him, keep feeling him. Little trickles of rainwater dotted his cheekbones. She moved her hand to his face and wiped them away as he had wiped hers.

He frowned, his eyes growing darker, then bent again to touch her lips. This time, he knew, she was ready. This time when he flicked his tongue gently over her parted lips, he felt her tremble, but she returned the kiss. The strange new feelings, the unusual current of electricity so strong between them, was no longer a surprise. He knew he had to keep tasting her, the need kept building within him to feel her silky skin next to him.

Allie loved kissing him. He tasted of chocolate and coffee, she decided, and smelled of clean male scent blended with fresh air. The rain beat against the window, the pattering melding with her own heartbeat and back again. Her thumbs caressed the planes of his face. Eyes closed, she listened to the pounding of the raindrops and her heart. And when his lips moved to her cheek the feel of his mouth slipping sensuously along her wet skin made her shiver.

He moved slowly, as if making the most of every second, slowing down time with every move, with every breath. And when he was through caressing her skin with his lips, she held her breath, waiting, hoping his mouth would demand hers again, wondering what her reaction would be if it did.

She took a shaky breath as his lips dipped into the neckline of her T-shirt. She trembled and whispered, "Michael."

He stopped and lifted his head to kiss a raindrop from her ear. "You taste like summer," he murmured into her hair.

"Michael," she began again. What was she going to say to him? Common sense fought through tangled emotions. Their closeness was affecting her thinking. Had she ever felt this way with Paul? It had been so long ago she couldn't remember. How would she feel when Michael left? But what if he stayed, asked a little hopeful voice.

He dropped his hands from her face and held her loosely by the shoulders. "Isn't this the time when you tell me we shouldn't be doing this?" He kissed her lightly and backed away, holding her hands. "You're supposed to tell me to stop, that I'll be leaving soon, that this is something neither one of us needs." He squeezed her hands, smiling gently into her upturned face.

"Even if you're right, are you speaking for me," she asked carefully, "or for yourself?"

He sighed, his face serious and older looking than a few moments before. "Both, I suppose."

"What happened to you, Michael?" She sensed he'd been hurt. And she knew she was right.

He shook his head. "Not important." The last thing he wanted to do tonight was discuss the past. He felt as if it was a century ago and wished he never had to think about it at all.

"Why not?"

He stepped away from her. "Because I don't need your sympathy and I don't want your—" he hesitated "—affection."

She struggled to lighten her words. "Just my body, huh?"

He grinned. "Yeah. How am I doing?"

"You tell me."

At the silent question in her eyes, his voice grew serious again. "I might hurt you when I leave, and staying is something I've promised—" He paused thoughtfully and rephrased it. "I don't have a lot to give."

She looked up into his strong, handsome face, at the depth of feeling he was trying to control. She remembered his thoughtfulness, his gentle humor, his kindness to her family. And his passion. He had so much to give. He had already shared a great deal with the people she loved. "You're so wrong, Michael."

He protested with a shake of his head.

She touched his face lightly. "Have it your way, my friend." Turning away, she took the flashlight off the counter. "Good night," she said, and smiled. "I'll leave you the candles." She walked carefully up the stairs, her thoughts running helplessly around inside her head. She told herself she was relieved, that she didn't need the clumsy burden of making love coming between them all week. She reminded herself of all her fears about becoming involved. That was a long list, and by the time she crawled into bed and hugged the covers for warmth she was almost convinced it was better to remain alone. Hours later, when the digital clock on the dresser began to blink, and the electricity was restored, Allie was still awake.

6

"WE'VE TAKEN A VOTE," Danny announced importantly the next morning, breaking into the loud whirring of Allie's sewing machine as she guided the material through the needle.

Allie lifted her foot from the pedal, silencing the machine temporarily, but she kept her hands on the flowered fabric. It was good to keep busy. There would be another quilt to sell Saturday if she could just keep her mind on sewing and her thoughts away from her houseguest. His sleeping bag had disappeared from the living room by the time she'd come downstairs this morning and she assumed he'd moved back to the tent when the storm was over.

"Fix peanut butter sandwiches, Dan. You can eat in the playhouse, if you want." She pressed the pedal again, anxious to have the long seams finished by noon. The sun was heating her back despite the protection offered by the miniblinds that shaded the windows.

"That's not what I'm talking about!" Dan protested.

"We had a better idea," rumbled Michael from the doorway.

Allie paused again, frowning slightly as she studied the eager intruders. Sherry and Glen were radiating excitement, and Dan looked anxiously at Michael. He was calm, his brown eyes meeting her steadily, allowing no embarrassment from last night to enter. Allie switched off the sewing machine and leaned back in her chair. "Okay, I give up. What's going on?"

"Fishing!" Glen squeaked. The others nodded.

Michael continued, "I thought I might as well see a little of the lake while I'm here. I jogged down to the marina this morning and rented a boat from Fred, so we're all set."

"We are?" she echoed doubtfully.

"Well, you don't have to come if you don't want to, but I thought the kids might enjoy doing some fishing with me."

She looked back at the children, who were practically bursting with joy at the thought of spending the rest of the day on the lake. How could she say no? Yet Michael knew damn well she wasn't going to let her children go off in a boat with someone who had never been out on the lake before. How would she know they'd be safe? She glanced at the unfinished seams rippling down to her lap. There was a lot of work left to do. How could she say yes?

"Say yes and I'll buy lunch. We'll eat on the boat," he cajoled. "Besides, Allie, this room is going to be an oven in another hour and you won't be able to work here anyway."

The children were holding their breaths. She knew Michael was right, so she gave in gracefully. "Okay, you win. But *you*—" she looked at the kids "—have to dig the worms."

They cheered and ran to get into their bathing suits. Dan gave instructions to the younger ones as they left the room. It was obvious he didn't want anything to go wrong with the fishing trip.

"Thanks," Michael said, smiling as if she had done him a favor. "I haven't been fishing in years." He drew up a chair at the table and sat down near her. "And it's no fun to go alone."

"Don't thank me yet," she said, laughing. "You may change your mind after this afternoon. I hope you don't end up throwing us all overboard! We're awfully noisy fishermen."

He chuckled. "I can imagine. But it doesn't matter."

"I'll remember you said that." She lifted the strips of fabric from her lap and piled them on the table.

"Tell me about this craft show. Is it in Hope?"

"No," she said, surprised at his interest. It had been such a sore subject yesterday. "It's in Sandpoint, part of the annual beach barbecue and art show." She stood up and stretched. "It's really grown in the past few years, from a local event to a huge show that attracts crafts people and tourists from all over the Northwest."

"How much do you have to have done by. . . when? Saturday?"

"Oh, I probably have enough already." She smiled, looking at him over the mounds of pillows she'd stuffed earlier that morning. "Want to see?"

"I'd like that."

She took him into the sewing room and opened a closet. Carefully she brought out her multiprint pictures, whimsical landscapes fashioned from fabrics and detailed with embroidered accents.

He picked one out and held it up. "It's beautiful, Allie."

"Thank you." She was pleased by his reaction. The loving creation of these pictures had filled a long winter. She hoped that someday she would get a good price for this kind of work.

"You really are an artist," he said, examining some of the others. "Have you sold many of these yet?"

"No. This will be the first show for them. I'm making quilts and pillows in a last-minute panic. I'm afraid if these pictures don't sell I won't make enough money—" She broke off, reluctant to bring up the subject of finances again.

But he was engrossed in the pictures, one in particular. "I know someone who would love this one."

She stepped closer, curious to see which picture he held, but Dan came racing into the room. "C'mon, Mom, before it gets too late!"

Michael took him by the shoulders and marched him out of the door, laughing. "Give your mother a break and show me where we're going to dig worms."

Allie tucked her pictures back into the closet and then went to the kitchen to pack a picnic. She wasn't going to let Michael buy lunch after his bringing home all those groceries yesterday. She tossed an assortment of cookies, potato chips, cheese and the last slices of leftover cheesecake into the cooler. She was spreading mustard on bologna sandwiches when she heard Michael calling.

She went to the back door and looked out. "What?"

Michael leaned on the shovel handle. "The kids want to show you how many they've dug up!"

Opening the door she made her way up the steps and over to the unused garden filled with worm diggers.

"See, Mom?" Glen tipped a coffee can at a perilous slant to show her the wiggling dirt inside.

"Gee, nice work," Allie said, taking a step backward.

Glen pulled a thick curling worm from the can, dangling it in front of Sherry. She frowned, and peered carefully through the ground Michael had just overturned with his shovel. "Oooh! Bunches!" she shrieked, reaching to grab a mass of tangled worms in both hands. Her eyes widened as she spotted more. Allie and Michael chuckled in unison at the frustration on the small child's face when she realized her hands were too full to grab another worm.

In desperation she started to tuck the worms under her armpit for safekeeping.

"No!" Allie cried, trying to keep the laughter out of her voice. Sherry's feelings were hurt easily if she thought anyone was laughing at her.

Michael choked out, "Glen or Dan, share the cans with your sister." To Allie he said, "She's a character, isn't she? I have a sister who used to do things like that when she was little."

"Where is she now?" It was the first time he'd mentioned his family, and she was curious.

"Seattle. Married, with twin girls." He bent over to move some rocks out of the way of the digging. "Guess we'd better finish this job."

She hesitated before going back into the house. The blue sky was clear and bright. The only reminder of last night's storm was the missing layer of dust off the truck. It was too beautiful a day to waste behind a sewing machine. Suddenly she wanted the afternoon to be special. "You're going to need a fishing license. And I think we'd better rent some more poles. I just have a couple of old ones up in the garage."

He grinned at her. "I did all that this morning, down at the marina."

It was easy to smile up into those gleaming brown eyes of his. "You were that sure you could talk me into going?"

"Let's just say I knew you were a woman who wasn't opposed to a little relaxation now and then."

THERE WAS SOMETHING magical about being out on the water. Allie was so comfortable she could hardly keep her eyes open.

The boat was much bigger than she'd expected. It must have cost Michael a small fortune to rent, but when she had questioned him he'd said he was more interested in safety than the cost. She couldn't argue with that, and was grateful the children were not in danger of falling out of the boat, despite the life vests they wore.

After lunch, Sherry had crawled under the shady V created by the bow of the boat and within minutes she had dozed off. Glen and Dan were more interested in eating cookies than watching the trolling lines attached to the back of the boat. They trailed their hands in the water and good-naturedly argued about who was eating the most cookies.

Michael pointed off to one side. "What are those mountains called?"

She raised her voice so he could hear over the engine. "The Green Monarchs. That's what you see out the living room window, beyond the peninsula."

"They look like they rise right out of the water."

"They do," she agreed, "but there are a few small beaches you can see when you get closer."

He lightly turned the steering wheel and they headed toward the mountains. "I could use a swim. How about you?"

He peeled off his T-shirt, revealing a broad expanse of chest. Allie was grateful for the sunglasses that hid her eyes, leaving her free to admire those muscles. A floppy white hat shaded her face. "Definitely," she replied.

"I'd better reel the lines in, then. You want to take the wheel?" He thought she looked cute in that hat and he wished he was alone with her. But after last night he knew how dangerous that could be.

"Sure." She moved to the driver's seat, and her legs brushed against his briefly. He eased his way to the back of the boat, grabbing a cookie from Danny before unhooking the fishing pole.

When they came within sight of a beach, Michael took control of the wheel again, directing the boat slowly into a tiny deserted bay. Allie and the boys hung their heads over the side, on the lookout for submerged boulders that could damage the boat's propeller. But Michael avoided the rough spots easily and coasted the boat into shore after killing the engine.

"Nice landing, Captain," she said.

He gave her a quick salute, then climbed over the side and scraped the boat's bow gently onto the beach. He tied its rope to an overhanging tree while the boys scrambled into the water and splashed enthusiastically. Allie shooed them away from the boat and their sleeping sister, then eased into the cool water to join them.

Michael dived expertly and swam a few hundred feet. She watched him before wading to the shore. The air smelled like pine needles. She sat on the edge of the shore, her feet in the shallow water while she sifted through the smooth thin rocks looking for arrowheads. Sometimes, if she was lucky, she'd find a trace of the Indian culture that had been so much a part of Idaho's history.

She glanced up at the boys from time to time. Michael was showing Dan how to do the backstroke; Glen was content with the dog paddle. The three of them looked like they were having a great time.

Michael emerged from the lake, his hair slicked back and his large body glistening in the sun. When he sat down beside her, spattering drops of water, Allie suddenly felt shy. Memories of last night's kiss came rushing back, and embarrassment over her response washed over her. She wished she hadn't left her hat and sunglasses in the boat. What on earth was the matter with her? She knew she should get out more, find some outside interests. Maybe she should stop sitting on hot rocks.

"What have you been doing?" he asked curiously, crossing his arms casually over his bent knees. "Every time I looked, you were digging through the rocks."

"Arrowheads," she explained. "I just can't seem to stop looking, especially when I'm lucky enough to get out here on the lake." She kept sifting through the rocks, although not concentrating as she had been. "The Indians used to come from Montana, in the summer, to camp and pick berries. And make arrowheads."

"And where are they now?"

"There are reservations east of here, near Missoula. But I'd rather picture what it must have been like around here hundreds of years ago."

He looked out over the sparkling blue water toward Hope. "I'll bet it didn't look much different then. You're lucky to live here."

"There must be advantages to living in a city, too," she offered.

He looked down at her. "Sometimes." He tried to picture Allie living in a city, but couldn't. She seemed to belong in this unspoiled part of the country.

"How do you know so much about fishing?" She stopped rearranging the beach and leaned back on her elbows.

"My father used to take us."

"Us?"

"My sisters and me."

"Are you the oldest?" Somehow she pictured him as a big brother, bossing his sisters around and being treated like a king.

He grinned. "Nope. The middle child, just like Glen. My older sister pushed me around, still does, actually. And the youngest tagged along after me and copied everything I did. But they were both better fishermen than I was."

"And your parents?" she asked. What would it have been like to grow up with a mother and father? It wasn't the first time she'd wondered about that.

"They're retired now. Dad worked for the railroad, and Mom was—still is—a writer, which is why my father took us fishing so often. She needed the extra hours to work. Now Dad's trying to make a fisherman out of *her*."

"Do they live in Portland?"

He nodded, leaning back along the rocky beach to lie beside Allie. "The sun feels good." He groaned, closing his eyes. She thought he had forgotten her question until he continued, "Mom and Dad still have the house we grew up in, but now they like to travel around in their motor home. I'll have to tell them about Hope when I get back."

The boys bounced out of the water and began to explore the shore, excited about finding rocks and driftwood to take home with them.

Michael's voice broke into the comfortable silence. "What about your family, Allie? Did you grow up here?"

She thought he had fallen asleep. "No. Farther south. I never knew what happened to my parents. I was raised in foster homes. Lots of them, in fact." She spoke quietly, keeping any trace of emotion from her voice. It had been such a long time ago—a lifetime, really.

He rolled on to his side, propping up his head with one hand. "I'm sorry. My—I knew someone once who grew up that way." He frowned, his thoughts far away. "She couldn't cope with any kind of family life at all. I guess because she'd never known the real thing."

"Well, it's not an easy way to grow up," she said softly. The sadness in his voice disturbed her. Was he talking about someone he'd loved?

"But you survived," he insisted. Didn't she know how lucky she was? "You're happy. You've made a home for yourself and your children."

She sat up and clasped her hands in front of her knees, hesitating before answering. "Every person is different, Michael. *Because* I grew up the way I did, I'd do anything for those kids. Anything to keep them safe and happy."

"Sometimes," he said heavily, "no matter how hard you try, that's impossible." And he was walking proof, he thought, no longer willing to continue the conversation. He stood up and called the boys. "C'mon, we've got some serious fishing to do today!"

When Michael automatically held out his hand to help Allie she grasped it firmly, grateful for the small courtesy.

"Michael," she began, starting to ask him what he meant.

He shook his head. "Forget I said that. It's too beautiful a day to spoil with such serious subjects." He looked over the top of her head, then whispered in her ear, "And if there weren't three pairs of eyes on us right now I'd be tempted to kiss that frown away."

Allie hoped she wasn't blushing. She definitely wasn't frowning any longer. "Three pairs?"

He straightened, then pointed behind her. "Sherry's waving at us from the boat. I'll go make sure she doesn't fall out."

"I'll round up the boys." But she didn't move right away. Instead she watched Michael as he waded through the shallow water toward the boat. Allie's small daughter lifted her arms to reach for him, trusting he would catch her as she tilted toward him.

Allie bit her lower lip, remembering leaning into Michael's arms last night. Had her expression been as trusting? She swallowed the lump in her throat. Maybe it's time, she thought. Time for the children to have a father, time for their mother to begin believing in happy endings.

She turned away and called the boys. Who was she kidding? Michael was a very special man, rapidly becoming a friend. *Only* a friend. There wouldn't be time for anything more than that.

7

"DO YOU HAVE any of these in gray?" A silver-haired woman in a lavender sundress pulled a patchwork pillow from the display basket and surveyed it critically.

Allie smiled politely and shook her head. "I'm sorry. I sold the gray one an hour ago. Would you like to order one?"

"Oh, no, thank you, dear. We're going back home tomorrow." She handed the rose-print pillow to Allie. "I'll just take this one."

Allie slipped the pillow into a plastic bag, accepted the woman's twenty-dollar bill and made change from a small metal cash box. The woman thanked her and moved on to a nearby display of pottery.

The supply of pillows was dwindling—an encouraging start to the first day of the craft show. It was almost lunchtime and customers had been keeping Allie busy since the fair began. Which was good, she thought, as she tucked the cash box under the card table and rested her sandaled feet on it for safekeeping. She'd had no time to think about Michael. He was wandering around there somewhere, after having helped her set up her display. That morning he had insisted on coming along, easily assembling the backdrop from which she'd hung her fabric pictures. Afterward he'd brushed aside her thanks and disappeared. She searched for him in the crowd and was angry with herself for the disappointment she felt when she didn't see him.

There were a lot of familiar faces among the entrants. Some she had traded with other years and at the Christmas bazaar last October. The elderly lady with the home-made dolls was directly across the lawn from her. She waved and Allie waved back. She might buy a doll for Sherry if sales continued as well as they had this morning.

She occupied a good position this year: a corner that jutted into the array of half-circles that looped around the grassy acres in front of the Sandpoint city beach.

"How's it going?" Barbara called, children trailing behind her as she approached Allie's table. "This heat is getting to us."

"I heard someone say it was almost a hundred degrees out here," Allie agreed, looking sympathetically at the children's red faces.

"Are you making lots of money, Mom?" asked Danny.

"Enough to treat you all to Popsicles." She mentally counted the money in her head, adding up the totals of four pillows and one pastel baby quilt. The fabric pictures had received a lot of favorable comments, but so far no one had purchased one. It was still early, she reminded herself, but she prayed she hadn't gotten her hopes too high about her new venture.

She was reaching for the cash box when Barbara said, "Save your money. I think we'll just head back to Hope and go swimming. Why don't you let the kids spend the night at my house? Ron's promised to set up the tent for the boys, and Tina can keep Sherry out of trouble."

The children cheered the idea, but Allie questioned her friend. "Have you lost your mind?"

Barbara shrugged. "I still owe you for when you had my three kids while Ron and I were in Mexico. Let me work off a little guilt, okay?"

Allie smiled. It was hard to argue with her friend's logic, although she suspected Michael's presence had something to do with Barbara's offer. She couldn't help wanting to further a romance and was doing it the only way she knew how. "I can see right through you."

Barbara winked. "C'mon, troops, we're off." She pointed to the parking lot. The kids waved goodbye, forgetting all about Popsicles. Barbara called over her shoulder, "I offered Michael a ride home, but he said he'd go home with you later. Have fun!"

Allie waved weakly. She'd been set up. A group of gray-haired ladies arrived, paused to admire her work, and after a few smiles at Allie, moved past.

"There's so much to see," one lady said to another, fanning herself with her hat.

"Let's get something cold to drink and come back. I'm too hot to look anymore," another suggested.

Allie smiled sympathetically. Perspiration trickled from underneath her hat as she surveyed the crowd drifting through the craft fair. Most of them wore shorts or bathing suits, but their red faces reflected the effects of the relentless summer sun. She slumped in the seat, glad her long hair was tucked securely in a bun under the wide-brimmed hat. She had no idea the fetching picture she made, her tanned oval face highlighted by the cool flowered blouse, as she sat surrounded by colorful fabric prints and a soft daffodil tablecloth. When she grew tired of sitting, she walked around the table and readjusted the pictures with a critical eye.

"I'll take that one."

Allie turned to see Michael solemnly pointing to the picture of the lake with its jaunty green calico islands in the bay. She laughed. "Are you serious?"

"Of course," he said, pulling his wallet out of the back pocket of his tan slacks. "That's the one I liked the other day. Put a Sold sign on it." He smiled, that slow smile of his she found so appealing.

"Put your money away, Michael. We'll settle up later. Are you sure? How are you going to get it to Portland?" She sat back down in the chair, a little flustered with his purchasing the picture.

"I'll have it shipped." He made himself comfortable on the grass near her. "Your booth looks great. I've been all through the show. You don't have any competition."

"Thanks. Are you having a good time?" She noted his dark hair curled damply on his forehead. He probably wished he'd brought a bathing suit with him.

"Well, I haven't bought any pottery or sheepskin mittens, if that's what you mean. Just people-watching, mostly." He seemed distracted, looking around at the crowd, then turning back to Allie, as if remembering she was there. "Are you okay? You're not going to pass out from sunstroke, are you?"

She shook her head, "But the heat's awful, isn't it?" She reached under the skirted table for the cooler. "Want a cold drink? I packed a lunch, but it's too hot to eat."

"No, thanks. I had some sort of health food sandwich at one of the stands. I came to ask you if you wanted me to get you anything."

"Thanks, but this is all I need." She snapped the top from a diet cola and took a long swallow.

"Why don't you go for a swim?" he offered. "I'll watch the booth for you."

She choked on the soda. The thought of that burly football coach selling handmade quilts was too much for her.

"It's not that funny," he protested. "I'll charm the ladies."

"Yes," Allie drawled, "I'll bet you could do that just beautifully."

He stood up, slipped his hands into his pockets and looked sideways at her in mock disapproval. "I don't like the way you said that."

She had to laugh. "It was a compliment. Honest!"

He raised both eyebrows, his eyes twinkling mischievously. He looked as if he was about to tease her when her bearded neighbor began beating his bongo drums.

"How can you stand it?" Michael asked in a low voice.

Allie glanced at the thin young man who sat cross-legged on a Navaho blanket. He seemed to be in a trance as he beat the drums to some kind of inner music. "Oh, That's Jeremy. His music doesn't bother me."

"Music?" he echoed doubtfully. "Does he sell a lot of drums this way?"

"No. Handmade jewelry boxes. It's a lot better than having the Ka-Flooey man next to me," she assured him, remembering last year's noisy neighbor. His distracting display of dancing figures on sanded sticks had fascinated young and old, luring her potential customers away before they'd even had a chance to look at her quilts.

"The what man?" He frowned, turning back to her.

"Never mind," she said. "Go take a look at the boxes. They're pretty unusual."

Michael seemed skeptical, but casually wandered over. Pretty soon he and Jeremy were deep in conversation. The drumming had ceased while they talked, and Allie's attention was drawn to a wealthy-looking couple who wanted to purchase a quilt. They were eager to order a custom-made one, so by the time Allie had taken all the information and a deposit, Michael was gone again.

The bongo rhythm continued softly.

"Jeremy?" she called.

"Hmm?"

"Where'd he go?"

Jeremy looked up, squinting against the sunlight. "Your friend? That guy?"

She nodded.

"Said to tell you—" thump, thump "—he'd be back in a while—" thud, thud "—after the puppet show."

"Oh, thanks." Why would Michael want to see that? Oh, well. She didn't pretend to understand everything he did. And the entertainment planned at the makeshift center stage was designed to attract people of all ages. She wished the children could have stayed to see it, despite the heat.

She shifted uneasily on the kitchen chair she had brought to the fair. The heat grew worse, and most of the crowd drifted off toward the lakefront. She didn't blame them. She'd rather swim than shop on a day like this, too. The afternoon dragged on. Jeremy softly pounded his drums; the pottery people on the other side of her hid in their air-conditioned motor home.

Allie was lonesome. She munched on an apple and tried to catch sight of Michael's tall form. She hated to admit that she missed him, but she did. He was filling up her life and she didn't know what to do about it. Ever since the phone call from his friend Jake, who had said the bike was on its way, she had waited uneasily for its arrival. And for Michael's departure. Sometimes she hoped it would never come. She smiled to herself, remembering Barbara's advice to smash every bike until he got the message and stayed. Why couldn't life be simpler? She tossed the apple core back into the cooler. Why couldn't she just say, "Stay.

I want to know you better. There's something here between us and I'd like to give it a chance."

But what if he didn't feel the same way? What if he was always nice to divorcées and children? What if his calm acceptance of his time with them was just his way of reacting to an unusual situation?

She frowned, absently fanning herself with a folded paper bag. There had to be women—or a woman—in his life. He radiated sex appeal, in that strong-silent-type way of his. Who was waiting in Portland? Had he sent her postcards? Had he called her from the pay phone in front of the Hope Market? He'd been married once, at least he'd admitted that, although she'd had to drag it out of him. But it hadn't been a happy marriage, Allie guessed. It was easy to recognize the symptoms. She should know, after all.

"Jeremy? Would you watch my table for a few minutes?" She'd take a walk, she decided, visit the rest room, see if she could find a breeze near the water.

On her way back to her table, she saw Michael talking to the Montana "cookbook people" near their converted school bus. She waved to him, but he didn't see her. He looked very serious, even from a distance.

"Thanks," she told Jeremy. "Any business?"

He shook his head. Allie took her place behind the table just as some people wandered by and she was kept busy for a while discussing her pictures and quilts. There was no time to wonder about Michael Rhodes.

He sauntered toward her later on, when many of her fellow exhibitors were covering their wares with sheets and blankets. Allie looked up from her packing when he called her name.

"You're not going to leave these things here, are you?" he asked, noting other people walking away for the night.

She shook her head. "No. It isn't hard to take them home and set up again tomorrow. I'll leave the table, though."

"Did you have a profitable day?"

She wondered if her face looked like a ripe tomato. She slipped some ice chips from the cooler and wiped her face. "Yes. Better than I'd expected."

"Good. Then we can celebrate with dinner."

"Oh, I don't think—"

"In an air-conditioned restaurant?"

It was a tempting idea. "You're feeding me again," she protested feebly.

He touched the reddened tip of her nose. "Call it first aid."

"Right, Doctor. Call it anything you want, it sounds good to me." She reluctantly stepped away from his touch and reached for her purse and the cash box. Michael carried the rest of her things to the truck, where they were stored in the front seat. Allie hid the cash box under the seat and locked the doors.

Michael took her hand. "Let's walk. There's a place nearby I want to try. I like this town—you can walk just about anywhere."

"You sure have found your way around in a hurry," she observed, trying to keep up with his long strides.

He slowed down, squeezing her hand lightly. "I'm trying to impress you."

"You don't have to impress me." She looked up at him, expecting to see the teasing smile on his face. But he looked serious again. At least he wasn't smiling.

They walked in silence to the restaurant, and he hustled her through a large oak-trimmed glass door into the cool foyer of the Greenhouse restaurant.

"I've never been in here before," she said, noting the tiled floor and dark paneling, wondering if her wrinkled clothing was too casual.

"I saw it from the beach today. There's a dining room that faces the lake."

The hostess greeted them politely. "Two for dinner?"

Michael nodded. "Yes. Something overlooking the water." He wouldn't have many more days to enjoy the view of the lake, Michael thought. Or to enjoy Allie's company.

"Fine." The hostess smiled. "Would you like to wait in the lounge until we have a table ready?"

Michael looked down at Allie. She looked as if she was starving, and he remembered she'd refused his offer of lunch. "Okay with you?"

"It sounds heavenly," she agreed, gazing down into a sunken lounge area that held assorted celery-green wing chairs, love seats and blue Oriental rugs. A massive chandelier hung from a glass-domed ceiling, and a polished black grand piano stood elegantly in one corner of the cool room.

They found two velvety chairs in a secluded corner and ordered margaritas from the cocktail waitress. Delicious aromas mingled with the tinkle of glassware and the low hum of conversation that surrounded Allie and Michael.

"This is better than Jeremy's drums," Michael said contentedly. His large body filled the wing chair. His long legs were less than an inch from Allie's skirted knees and she had no desire to move away.

Allie felt herself relaxing now that she was finished with the day at the craft show. She massaged one temple. "I think it was finally getting to me. I'll have to brace myself for tomorrow." She removed her hat and attempted to smooth the sides of her hair, suddenly realizing what she must look like. "Excuse me, Michael. I'd better go put myself back together."

"You look fine just the way you are. You always do." From the skeptical expression on her face, he knew she didn't believe his words. He smiled at her, insisting. "Really."

"Thanks, but I'll be right back." Flustered by his compliment, she grabbed her purse and went to find the powder room. *You like him too much,* she told the sunburned face in the mirror. She pulled the elastic from her hair and brushed the tangles into soft waves that fell to her shoulders. She splashed water on her face and dried it with a paper towel. Then Allie straightened her blouse, wanting to look her best. How many times did she get an invitation to eat at the Greenhouse? She told herself her pleasure had nothing to do with the man who was waiting for her in the lounge.

An icy drink sat on the oval table beside her chair. Michael reached over and handed it to her when she sat down. He clinked their glasses together. "To profit."

"Amen," she answered, sipping from the salty rim of the margarita glass. "This is wonderful." Allie took several long swallows.

"You'd better be careful," he said. "Did you eat anything today?"

She shook her head, and sipped more of her drink. "Too hot." The crushed ice felt delicious as it cooled her parched throat.

"Take it easy with that, then. I don't want to have to carry you out of here before dinner." He glanced around the room impatiently, then smiled. "I'm starving."

Allie finished her drink and signaled the waitress for another by raising her empty glass. This was a wonderful restaurant, she decided, as the waitress appeared with a refill. "Another for you, sir?"

"No. One of us has to drive home." His tone was mild.

"Nice to have you around, Mike," Allie replied gaily.

Michael ignored the unsanctioned use of his name, a smile threatening his lips. "You don't have to gulp it, you know. We have plenty of time."

Plenty of time? She shook her head. He was so wrong. "Oh, no. We don't." She couldn't believe she had said that. It just slipped out. She looked away from his dark eyes, thinking she'd have to be more careful. An empty stomach and a minor case of sunstroke didn't mix with alcohol.

He answered quietly, "I know. And you'll never know how sorry I am about that."

"Then why don't you tell me?" She surprised herself with the question. But she needed answers. Was their attraction to each other a hopeless dream on her part? Or was there something special that only needed time and nurturing to blossom? She looked at him until he brought his gaze to meet hers.

His voice was guarded. "I don't think so."

"I guess I don't understand you. And why should I? You've never shared much of yourself." She sipped the drink slowly. "By the way, I thought you were anxious to get on the road. You were upset about your trip being delayed when I ran over your bike, and since then you've made yourself at home."

"You've made it easy to stay."

"That's not an answer." She sighed, tired of word games.

"But I do have to leave soon." He said it quietly, with an absolute finality that struck Allie's heart.

"I thought so," she murmured. Suddenly the room wasn't quite so beautiful, nor the evening so perfect. There was nowhere to look, and she wondered if any of the misery she was trying to hide showed on her face.

The silence grew awkward, but she fought with herself against asking him to stay, compromising on what she hoped was a casual, "What's your hurry?"

He looked at her thoughtfully, a tender expression mixing with the resolution in his voice. "There's some business in Montana I have to take care of."

"Is there anything I can do to help you?"

"You already have. And you don't even know how, do you?" He smiled at her confused expression. How could he ever explain to her how much this past week had meant to him? "Let's have dinner. The hostess just waved to us."

He stood up and she rose shakily. Suddenly her knees felt as if they'd disappeared.

He took her elbow. "Let me help you. You're a cheap drunk, you know that?" he whispered affectionately in her ear. "We'd better get some food into you before you pass out."

She didn't bother to argue with him because he was right. The room was spinning slightly, just as his words spun in her head. What was she missing? There were pieces of a puzzle she hadn't been able to put together yet.

He guided her into the dining room to a table overlooking the lake. Colorful sailboats shared the bay with windsurfers. Allie and Michael ordered quickly from the oversize menus placed before them, opting for broiled lake-fresh trout. She had to blink several times before the fuzzy edges disappeared from her line of vision. Her cheekbones felt numb, and she touched her face to make sure she was all in one piece.

Moments later, when the waitress arranged plates of leafy salad in front of them, Allie sipped from her water glass and prayed she wouldn't collapse under the table. She picked up her fork and attempted conversation. "Did you buy a Montana cookbook today?"

Michael looked over at her, puzzled. "A what?"

"I saw you talking to the people who wrote it, the ones in the school bus," she prompted.

His face closed, wary. "No. I didn't." He stabbed at his salad and looked away from Allie.

Another puzzle piece, but where would she put it? "Does that have anything to do with your business in Montana?"

"You don't forget much, do you?"

"I'm determined to understand you," Allie replied cheerfully. Then she picked up her fork, rearranged the lettuce on the plate and halfheartedly stabbed a cherry tomato.

His voice rumbled, "Maybe there's not that much to understand."

"There's a game I used to play as a kid." She watched his relieved expression when he thought she was changing the subject of the conversation. "It goes something like this: I tell you a secret about myself and you tell me a secret about *yourself*." She watched as he finished the last of his salad and pushed his plate aside. "You weren't kidding about being hungry, were you?"

"Are you going to eat that?" He looked pointedly at her uneaten salad.

"No. Here." She put her fork aside and pushed the plate across to him. Sharing plates was something married couples did, people who'd been together for a long time. How could she and Michael be so easy with each other sometimes? And yet there was the physical attraction between them that had caused her more than one sleepless night. There was nothing easy, she mused, about being around this man. "Want to play?"

"Maybe. What are the rules?" Michael could see that Allie wasn't going to give up easily. Well, that was something else they had in common.

"There aren't any rules," she replied, her eyes smiling a challenge. She waited as the waitress cleared their empty plates. "So, who goes first?"

"Your game, you start." He smiled, somewhat wickedly, she thought.

"Let's see." She paused, wondering what she could tell him. She uncovered a warm roll from the bread basket on the table and slowly buttered it.

"You're stalling."

"I'm just thinking." Her thoughts were definitely confused tonight and her face still felt numb from the effects of the margaritas. A secret—what would it be? She tried to remember the secrets she'd revealed when she'd played this game as a kid. "When I was a child, I pretended that Walt Disney was my *real* grandfather, and that I'd been kidnapped and never rescued so he didn't know where I was." She smiled ruefully at Michael across the table. "And every movie he made was really for me, hoping his granddaughter would see it and remember him."

Well, that hit close to home, Michael thought. He sat quietly, studying Allie's face for traces of bitterness. To his surprise, he found none. She seemed to find that memory amusing, and he wondered why. "That's a very sad secret."

"Oh, no," she said solemnly, but her green eyes twinkled. "Because when I married Paul, my ex-husband, I begged to go to Disneyland on our honeymoon, but I didn't tell him why. He thought I was crazy." Her laughter bubbled over, as she remembered Paul's expression.

"And did you go?" He wanted to hold her in his arms, but instead settled for reaching across the table and nestling her small hand inside of his.

She shook her head. "No. We went camping instead. But someday I'm going to take the kids there."

He squeezed her hand gently. "Yes, I'll bet you will."

Allie reluctantly pulled her hand away when their dinner was served. She tried not to remember the night of the storm and the way Michael's body had felt against hers. She looked away from him, down at her plate. The fish, surrounded by fresh vegetables, smelled delicious. And beside it, a huge baked potato cupped a pat of melting butter. She would concentrate on the food, she decided as she picked up her fork.

"Are you feeling all right?" There was concern in Michael's voice.

It was pleasant to be worried about, but rather embarrassing at the same time. "I think the drinks went to my head. I should know better than to drink on an empty stomach," she admitted sheepishly.

"Especially after sitting in the sun all day," he cautioned. "But was it worth it?"

"The show, you mean?" At his nod, she continued, "Oh, yes. There's a man from a gallery in Seattle who is interested in my pictures. He'd like to try some on consignment. He said 'country primitives' were very popular right now." She made a face. "A country primitive, that's me." The food was delicious, she thought. One hundred times better than hot dogs.

"Maybe you'll need to move to the city to market your work," he suggested, although he couldn't imagine her living anywhere else.

"I've thought about that sometimes. But I love the small-town life, too. I've never known anything else, really. I've often wondered what it would be like to live in a big city. I guess if I could, I'd have it both ways—the best of both worlds?"

"It's possible."

Smiling she shook her head. "Maybe. But for now I'm content with my life the way things are." Even as she said it, she knew it was no longer true. She *had* been content, until this man had rolled into her life and showed her what she was missing: someone to love, someone to return that love, someone to help, to lean on, to make love with. That last thought popped unbidden into her mind. Either her defenses were down, or else the alcohol was an aphrodisiac. *Watch it, Al,* she warned herself. Her face showed her feelings as clearly as a television broadcast.

No lovemaking, she told herself firmly as the waitress offered to remove their plates. "I'd like a cup of coffee, please" she told her.

Michael nodded. "Make that two. And a dessert menu."

"Mind reader." Allie laughed, and ordered a hot fudge sundae. Michael asked for apple pie. When dessert arrived, Michael ignored the pie in front of him, preferring to watch Allie. She'd dug into the oversize ice cream concoction with the same energy she seemed to devote to everything she did. Michael knew he hadn't played fair. Allie had let him into her life this past week and he kept shutting her out of his. He wanted everything his own way—taking all and giving nothing, he thought harshly. Typical. "Look at me," he demanded quietly.

She did. A fall of silky waves brushed her cheek and she absently tucked it behind one ear. "You're not getting my dessert, Mr. Rhodes."

"It's not your dessert I want, Mrs. Leonard," he murmured. She was beautiful, even with a sunburned nose. She could make him forget anything, even important

PLAY
HARLEQUIN'S

LUCKY HEARTS
GAME

AND YOU COULD GET

- ★ FREE BOOKS
- ★ A FREE MAKEUP MIRROR AND BRUSH KIT
- ★ A FREE SURPRISE GIFT
- ★ AND MUCH MORE!

TURN THE PAGE AND DEAL YOURSELF IN →

PLAY "LUCKY HEARTS" AND YOU COULD GET...

★ Exciting Harlequin Temptation® novels—FREE
★ A lighted makeup mirror and brush kit—FREE
★ A surprise mystery gift that will delight you—FREE

THEN CONTINUE YOUR LUCKY STREAK WITH A SWEETHEART OF A DEAL

When you return the postcard on the opposite page, we'll send you the books and gifts you qualify for, absolutely free! Then, you'll get 4 new Harlequin Temptation® novels every month, delivered right to your door months before they're available in stores. If you decide to keep them, you'll pay only $2.24 per book—26¢ less per book than the retail price—and there is no charge for postage and handling. You may return a shipment and cancel at any time.

★ Free Newsletter!

You'll get our free newsletter—an insider's look at our most popular writers and their upcoming novels.

★ Special Extras—Free!

You'll also get additional free gifts from time to time as a token of our appreciation for being a home subscriber.

things he wanted to say. Michael watched her eyes widen, then her lips tilted into a smile.

"Are you flirting with me again? I thought I warned you about that."

"I meant I wanted your attention."

"Oh, I think I understood you the first time," she said cheerfully. "Well, you have it for about ten seconds. I'm down to the second layer of fudge."

"I thought you wanted a secret," he explained, his voice teasing.

"I do." She took another bite of the ice cream coated with warm sauce.

Michael pushed his coffee cup aside and leaned toward her. He stopped the spoon's journey to Allie's mouth. "Please, don't lick that anymore." He smiled dangerously. "Or its effect on me won't be a secret."

The spoon clinked against the thick glass where she dropped it. She looked regretfully down at the melting mounds of ice cream and then back to Michael, meeting his gaze. "Seems a shame to waste it."

He chuckled and leaned back in his chair.

Heat warmed her cheeks when she realized what she'd said. "I didn't mean it that way." And then her laughter mingled with Michael's in the small corner of the room.

Michael signaled for the check. "I think we'd better go."

"Thank you," she told him, as they waited for the waitress to return. "Dinner was a wonderful idea, and totally unexpected."

His relaxed tone matched hers. "You're welcome. I enjoyed it. I don't get you to myself very often."

"Not many men date women with children," she mused. Oh, no, why had she referred to this evening as a date, for heaven's sake?

His eyebrows raised a fraction. "No? Since when?"

She was at a loss for words. "I know this isn't a date actually, but . . ."

The waitress returned his charge card and receipt. He slipped the card from the plate into his wallet and replaced it in his pants pocket. "Of course it is, and I'm glad." His smile caught her off guard.

"Me, too," she answered truthfully.

He stood up and held out his hand. "Ready?"

She put her hand in his, enjoying the warmth and strength of its clasp. They walked back to the truck in companionable silence, then Michael drove the twenty miles home. As the truck came to a stop in the driveway, Allie was acutely conscious that her children were not home. The house was uncharacteristically dark and she and Michael were alone. They were going to be alone all night.

Neither one moved to get out of the truck.

Michael brushed a curtain of silky hair from Allie's shoulder, enjoying the texture of it against the back of his hand.

"I shouldn't say this, but it's lovely being without the children for a change." She could feel his fingers teasing her neck and her spine turned to melted butter.

"Yes." He withdrew his hand from the softness of her hair and rested his arms on the steering wheel. "Being a single parent is a constant job. But I—"

He stopped suddenly and Allie caught an undercurrent in his voice. He hadn't said "must be" a constant job. He'd spoken as if he knew exactly what he was talking about. "But what?"

"But I loved it," he stated heavily. "I had a daughter, Allie, and she drowned several years ago."

"Oh, Michael, I'm sorry." The pain she'd seen in his eyes had not been imagined.

"I've accepted it—I had no choice—but a large part of my life went with her." He faced Allie in the darkness and touched her face. "I told you once that I didn't have a lot to give. But I'm hoping somehow this trip will remedy that. My life's been on hold for a long time." With a touch of surprise, he realized the healing had begun already.

"I don't understand, Michael." She still couldn't see how a biking trip would ease the grief of losing a child. She could only assume his daughter had died in Montana somewhere. Maybe he and his wife had divorced afterward. She'd heard of marriages breaking up that way. But she didn't want to pry any further. "Are you sure I can't help?"

"You have," he answered, his voice rich and warm. He cupped her chin and wished he could erase the pity from her eyes. "Don't look so sad. It happened a long time ago." His lips brushed hers until their breath mingled in the darkness and their bodies leaned toward each other. His hands found her face and combed through her hair, urging her closer through parted lips while the need to have her quickened inside of him. She tasted of fudge and cream and smelled like wildflowers. And if he didn't get control of himself he'd be attempting to make love to her on the front seat of a Datsun pickup truck like some kind of teenage animal.

"What's so funny?" Allie didn't know why he'd pulled away, but she heard his soft chuckle in the darkness.

"I am. I think we'd better go in."

She hopped out of the truck. The feeling of relaxation she'd enjoyed in the restaurant seemed very far away. "It's so quiet."

"I don't think I'll complain about it." He touched her back lightly as they walked down the dark steps to the kitchen door.

"I've wanted to do this all day." His lips met hers gently and the warmth of his body enfolded her as he backed her against the door. His hands caressed her shoulders through the thin cotton blouse, then slid slowly up to her nape to become entwined in the silky fall of hair. "It's been a long time since I kissed my date good-night at the door."

She tried to echo his teasing tone, but her voice quavered. "You certainly don't seem to be out of practice." Should she invite him in or would he mistake the offer for something else? She didn't know what she wanted, but she knew she didn't want the evening to end. "Coming in?"

He caressed her back, "Your little chaperons aren't here, Mrs. Leonard. And my control is shot all to hell. You'd better be sure about the invitation before you unlock the door."

That was the trouble, Allie knew. She wasn't sure about anything. She sensed his withdrawal even before he backed away and reached in his pants pocket for the keys.

He dropped them into her waiting palm, being careful not to touch her. A man could only take so much.

She realized that she'd hesitated too long when he turned away and walked to the side of the house toward his tent.

Allie slid the key into the lock, and opened the door. She didn't bother to turn on any of the lights, going directly upstairs to the shelter of her blue and white bedroom. The double bed looked rather forlorn. She turned her back on it and looked out the window toward the lake instead.

Her body was ready for more than Michael's kisses. No surprise there, since she'd practically dissolved onto the seat of the truck a little while ago. But was she ready emotionally for another attachment? Especially when, with her eyes wide open, she was practically issuing an engraved invitation to be hurt. "Ride right over me," she might as well advertise. "Go ahead, somebody. Hurt me again."

Still, he'd opened up to her tonight, telling her about his daughter. Her heart ached for him—what a father he must have been. But he could remarry, have a family...

She was falling in love with Michael Rhodes. It was a stupid, foolish, hopeless thing to do. Allie turned away from the window and pulled the curtains closed. She wouldn't think about him any more tonight.

She slipped a long peach cotton gown over her head, telling herself she was looking forward to going to sleep.

It had been such a long day, but a successful one as far as business went. She realized with a start she'd left the cash box in the truck. And the truck wasn't locked. The small town was practically crime-free but that was no reason to tempt fate. Even if the money *was* hidden under plastic bags of pillows. She sighed, and padded barefoot downstairs.

Allie opened the back door quietly, so she wouldn't disturb Michael, and quickly scurried up the steps to the truck. Quietly she opened the door, grateful for the tiny dome light illuminating the bundles. She rummaged quickly under the seat until she felt the cash box and pulled it toward her, then shut the door carefully. Moments later Allie approached the back door, the metal box tucked under her arm.

A shadow loomed against the corner of the house. "What the hell!" it roared.

She jumped, the cash box crashed to the ground and bounced open, money and change scattering on the grass.

"Allie?" The shadow came closer, turning into Michael. "What are you doing out here?" His chest was bare, his belt dangling unbuckled as if he had pulled on his pants in a hurry.

"I—I forgot the cash box," she stammered, trying to deal with the sudden rush of heat weakening her knees. It was easier to crouch on the lawn and gather money.

"I'm sorry I scared you." He knelt near her and searched in the grass for bills. "But you look like a ghost in that get-up."

"This is no getup—this is my nightgown." She pushed the money back into the box. It was embarrassing wondering how much of her body could be seen through the light cotton material. "I'll have to pick up the change in the morning."

He stood up. "I can do it now. Let me just get my flashlight."

"No!" The last thing she needed was light. She clutched the box to her, hoping her breasts were covered, and opened the kitchen door. "But thanks anyway."

There was laughter in his voice when he answered. "Are you sure?"

How could he be so casual when they were all alone and only partially dressed? She called good-night to him before shutting the door. She leaned against it for a long moment. There was no denying what she felt when she looked at him, or worse, when he took her in his arms.

The soft knock on the door vibrated between her shoulder blades like a massage, and she didn't hesitate this time to turn around and twist the doorknob. She pulled, he pushed, and the cooling night air seemed to bring him inside.

"I decided I couldn't wait for an invitation," he rumbled.

"You don't need one. Close the door."

He did. It was the softness in her voice that got to him. He couldn't take his eyes off her, afraid she would disappear into the night. Her body was a series of tantalizing shadows under her gown as he followed her up the stairs and into the large room at the end of the hallway. And when she turned around he pulled her to him, unable to resist touching her any longer.

"Why'd you change your mind?" He dragged his hands to her tiny waist, then below, to the enticing curve of her hips. His whisper was a tingling breath near her earlobe, jumbling her thoughts so she didn't know how to answer his question. She loved the strength of his body, hard against hers. Her hands skimmed along his waist and around to his muscled back while she tried to remember how to speak. Her knees trembled, and she hoped frantically he wouldn't notice. She didn't want him to know how much this meant to her. How much *he* meant to her.

"Oh, Allie, I've wanted you for so long," he whispered into her hair. His lips claimed hers with a kiss that held her thoughts spellbound while his hands brought her body alive.

He traced the delicate ribbon of her spine to her neck and down again, palming her buttocks with swirling motions as if he needed to assure himself she was really his. With a groan he buried his face in the warm hollow between her neck and shoulder, until his hands joined his lips in baring a trail of skin. He slipped the flimsy gown past her shoulders until, in frustration, she tugged it off her arms and let it slip forgotten to the floor.

Allie was not ashamed of her body. She stood before him and smiled as she reached to tangle her fingers in the mat of curling hair that coated his wide chest. "I've wanted to do this," she murmured, pressing her face against his heated skin. "And this." Her lips searched for the flat nipple and she flicked it delicately with her tongue before moving to the other.

His loose belt buckle tickled her stomach until she felt Michael's knuckles graze her skin while he unzipped his pants.

"I can't stand up anymore," she whispered, as he slipped off the rest of his clothes.

"Neither can I." His voice was rough and low. He tugged her toward the waiting bed. "Come here."

He pushed the quilted covers off the bed and pulled her onto the mattress with him. It was sweet relief, she thought, to let the bed support the weight of her melting body. She lay in a tangle of sheets facing Michael, not touching, but the small space between their bodies was electric with the knowledge of what was to happen.

And then he touched her. Trailing his index finger across her parted lips and down, between her tightening breasts, lingering to circle their aching tips.

"Beautiful," he murmured, and his lips continued the motion his finger had begun until Allie moaned from wanting him. His tongue sent shivers of need deep into her body, pleasure tugging her insides until she thought she would drown in it, until his hand continued its erotic journey and probed the softness between her thighs. He dipped into the moisture he found there and circled gently. Allie felt herself widen with the ache of needing more.

"Michael—"

"Shhh." He lifted his head to kiss her neck, licking the fragrant ridge of her collarbone before whispering in her ear, "I'm going to make love to you in all sorts of wonderful ways tonight, but first I need to feel you wrapped around me."

Allie wanted to touch all of him and moved closer until she felt the satin length of him brush her thigh. He was hot and hard against her. She wanted him inside of her, and slid her hand along his furred chest and down to brush his abdomen. She stretched her arm, trying to reach farther, and succeeded only in tormenting him with feather-light strokes that trapped him between her hand and her thigh.

He groaned, and moved to nudge Allie onto her back, as his fingers reluctantly slid from between her trembling thighs. He planted a hard kiss on her parted lips, then said, "Wait." The bed creaked as he eased away from her.

Aching and empty, she knew immediately why he was leaving. "You don't have to. It's—okay." She'd been taking the pill to regulate her cycle.

He hesitated. "Are you sure?"

"Yes."

He reached for her then, slipping alongside of her, setting fire to Allie's skin as he slid over her and nudged her legs apart. She was hot and pliant, welcoming and ready as he covered her with his body and braced his elbows on either side of her head.

She slid her hands to his waist and pressed the muscled ridge of his back with her palms, urging him closer. He bent his head to possess her lips, and she opened her mouth to his probing tongue. She felt her body's center melt as he moved his hips closer and eased himself against her, carving a moist hollow with the motion. She gasped at the size of him filling her, and their tongues met in the kiss, mouths sealed together as Michael's body penetrated completely. Allie couldn't think, could only feel, as Michael moved against her, pumping slowly, filling her again and again until she cried out against his mouth.

"You feel so good around me," he moaned against her lips as he quickened his thrusts. It was heaven to be inside her, and he knew he couldn't stop now. He could feel her tightening around him, pulling him deeper than he thought possible until he felt her explode beneath him. His body answered hers, shattering tremors shaking them both as they clung together.

He never wanted to let her go.

8

ALLIE WAS HAPPY. As the morning sun filtered through the bedroom curtains early Sunday morning that happiness filled her with all the sunshine in the month of July. She would have to enjoy this, she told herself as she stretched luxuriously under the cool cotton sheets. She would have to savor every drop of life-giving warmth, bask in each ray of heat that came from Michael's chocolaty eyes. It would be a long, cold and empty winter, but she didn't want to think about that. She wanted only to enjoy each summer day. Each summer day Michael was with her.

She was tempting fate. She knew it. Knew it as she threw back the covers. Knew it as she got out of bed and pulled on her sweatpants and shirt, brushed her teeth, combed her hair. With a delicious certainty she knew she could go downstairs, do her exercises and Michael would walk through the kitchen and lean against the doorjamb while she finished, a slow lazy smile on his rugged brown face.

She grabbed her sneakers and hurried downstairs. She didn't have to be in Sandpoint until ten o'clock, which gave her plenty of time. She wondered why she felt so energetic after making love with Michael for so long into the night. By rights she should be unconscious until noon.

When she saw him on the lawn doing some warming-up stretches she slipped quietly out the kitchen door to greet him. His smile warmed her right down to her suddenly trembling knees. She didn't know where and she didn't know when, but Allie was certain, as sure as God made Cheerios, Michael Rhodes was going to make love to her again.

She hoped it would be soon. She wished she didn't have to work today.

"Want to go with me?" he asked, jogging in place.

She swallowed hard. "I think so." Thank goodness he couldn't read her mind.

"Do you want to warm up first?" he panted.

"No. I think I've done that already." Just watching him made her heart pump faster.

"What's so funny?"

She shook her head. "Nothing. Let's go." She ran up the steps past him.

He caught up with her quickly, running easily beside her, adjusting his gait to match her small strides. "We'll take it slow." He looked down at her and grinned. "You're in great shape, but when you're not used to running you don't want to overdo it the first time."

"You're the expert," she agreed. "And you're right. I haven't done any, um, running for a long time." She concentrated on the mayor's flower garden, the barking terrier behind Mr. Gaither's fence, the new deck being built onto the yellow house on the corner. Barbara's house was quiet as they passed, but one of her neighbors was already out gardening and waved as Allie and Michael ran past.

"Who's that?"

"Grandma Baker. At least, that's what everyone calls her. I think she's been here since she was a little girl."

"What's her dog's name?" he asked.

"It died last fall, but she has a huge white cat called Feathers—" She stopped running and stood in the street. "Why are you laughing?"

"Sorry," he apologized through a chuckle. "But this is such a small town. Everyone knows the names of each other's *pets*." He took her elbow and nudged her into running again. "C'mon," he said, "you can tell me the name of the Irish setter that hangs out at the marina."

"All the way to the marina? Remember, I have to sell quilts in a couple of hours." And she still had to clean up, pick the loose coins off the grass, check with Barbara about the children and force herself to leave Michael and drive into town.

"I forgot about that." He jogged a half-circle around her and turned toward home. "There are other ways to exercise, Mrs. Leonard." He leered charmingly. "Follow me and I'll show you what I have in mind."

THE LAST DAY of the fair was as hot as the first one, but despite the heat Allie sold four pillows and two fabric pictures. It was an impressive showing, and one she was proud of. She was lucky, she thought, as she packed away her remaining pictures. She hadn't had to lower her prices. Many exhibitors slashed their prices during the last hours; nobody wanted to take home more merchandise than money.

"How'd you do today, Jeremy?" she called when she saw him set aside his drum and stand up to fold his blanket.

"Fair," he sighed, "just fair. This heat was a killer."

He quickly tucked the jewelry boxes into cardboard containers and was ready to leave. "See you at the Huckleberry Festival?"

She nodded. "Sure. Maybe by then I'll have made enough money to buy that blue-flowered jewelry box."

"I'll save it for you," he offered cheerfully. With a wink and a wave he was off toward the parking lot, and Allie finished dismantling her display.

She was wrestling with a jammed leg on the card table when a heavy-set man approached. His thick black beard touched an ancient flannel shirt, and suspenders stretched from black canvas pants to his burly shoulders.

"Hello," she said. "Can I help you?" He looked like a logger, she thought, as she waited expectantly.

"Mike here?" he boomed.

"Uh, no. Not today." How did this man know Michael?

He seemed stymied. "My old lady and me felt real bad we couldn't help that nice fella." He gestured toward the battered school bus across the lawn. "Well, you tell him Joe and Mattie said he's welcome to stop in anytime."

"I sure will." What on earth did he mean? She wanted to ask him what he was talking about, but before she could get the words out Joe was gone, heading back to his bus—the Montana Cookbook bus where she had seen Michael yesterday.

She started hauling her things to the truck. The cash box held more money today, making today's hours in town worthwhile. Driving away from Michael had been difficult, yet she had needed the distance between them. Things had been happening too fast, and that wasn't her style. Yet, it had felt so right. She should have been happy, but now there was an underlying sense of dread intruding upon her dreams. Michael had opened up last night, revealing part of his past. But there was more he wasn't telling her, she just knew it. It was almost as if something was closing in on her, she worried as she drove home later, something she didn't want to face. More missing pieces. What did she really know about Michael? His reasons for being in Idaho had been hazy, and she had no idea where he'd be right now if her truck hadn't run into his bicycle. For some reason that bothered her. Had she been too willing to let passion overrule common sense?

She stopped at a supermarket in town. She didn't want Michael to think she expected him to buy groceries all the time. By the time she parked her truck in her driveway, Allie was rumpled, sweaty and tired of worrying. That one night of lovemaking was not likely to be repeated, not with three children around and Michael leaving soon. And she would just have to try harder to think with her head instead of her heart.

It was time to be practical. She needed to call Barbara and have the kids sent home, then she wanted to stretch out in a lounge chair under the birch trees and feel the breeze from the lake. She wanted a large glass of iced tea and—

"Hey, Mom! Guess what?" Glen jumped up and down beside the truck.

"What? Move," she told the small boy, "so I can open the door." She stepped out of the truck and hugged her son. "What are you doing home? Did you have fun at Barbara's last night?"

"Yeah, but wait till you see what we're doin' in the playhouse." He took his mother's hand. "C'mon."

He dragged her across the lawn to the small building where Michael, Sherry and Dan were gathered. Sherry saw her first, breaking off the little tune she hummed to shout, "Mommy's home!"

Allie gave her a big hug. Michael looked up and put his hammer down. Dan grinned up at her, a small saw in his hand. "Hi, everybody. What's going on here?" She wished Michael would put a shirt on. A red bandanna tied around his forehead gave him a sexy look, Allie decided.

He grinned. "Can't you tell? We're making a safe place for Roady to have her kittens."

Glen's pregnant cat sat on the edge of the sandbox, surveying the proceedings with great interest. Sherry, holding a piece of sandpaper, went to sit beside her.

"I thought cats hid their kittens."

Glen tugged on her hand. "Well, when we find them we can put them in the playhouse so we can *see* them."

Michael gestured toward the lumber. "I hope you don't mind. I found some old boards and tools in the garage."

"Of course not. There was a lot of old stuff up there when we bought the place. You're welcome to anything you can find."

He grinned, a knowing look in his gleaming eyes. "I'll remember you said that. Tonight."

She stiffened. "I meant in the garage."

He chuckled. "I saw some screens in a corner. Do they belong to anything in particular?" He untied the bandanna and wiped the perspiration from his face and neck.

"No. Feel free to use them. Anything for Roady's comfort. Now—" she looked pointedly at her sons "—who's going to help me unload the truck?"

The kids groaned, and Michael answered, "We all will, Allie." He stood up, casually draping his arm across Allie's shoulders and steering her away from the children. "How'd it go today?"

She liked having his arm around her. It was such a friendly gesture. "Pretty good. But I'm glad it's over."

"Hey, Mom, did you buy us anything?" Dan called.

"Sure—lots of food!" His crestfallen face made her laugh. When they reached the truck she pawed through one of the bags. "Just kidding, Dan. There was a lady at the show who made lollipops out of fruit juice and I bought one for each of you." She passed them out to the kids.

"What about me?" asked Michael, standing very close to her. "Don't I get anything?" He grinned wickedly.

"You get to carry the groceries," she informed him, dumping a heavy brown bag into his arms. And I get to figure out what I'm going to do about falling in love with someone I hardly know.

It was dark, almost ten o'clock, before Allie's day was over. The children were in bed early, tired from a late bedtime the night before. Barbara had been thanked, sandwiches made for dinner, the groceries put away, leftover craft show merchandise piled in a corner of the living room. Allie sat in a mesh chair on the deck, her legs stretched out, feet propped on the deck's railing. She hadn't bothered to change out of the khaki shorts and flowered blouse she'd worn to the show.

"You look comfortable," Michael said from somewhere behind her.

She sighed contentedly. "I am. This breeze from the mountains is cooling me off."

"Tell me about your day. How was the show?" He pulled a chair next to hers and sat down, long legs propped against the railing.

"I did better than I thought I would. Sold two more pictures, among other things." She wiggled her toes, trying to ease the burning sensation.

"You have the smallest feet."

"What?" She looked at them critically, then at his. "Any feet would look small next to yours."

"Now, wait a minute," he replied in mock outrage, "I got these feet from my mother's side of the family." He obligingly slid one foot along the railing until it touched hers with a jolting sensual contact. Allie felt the tingling aftershocks throughout the most intimate parts of her body, and wondered how she thought she could control this man's effect on her. It was ridiculous to try, she decided, and let her legs stay casually on the railing. She was glad it was growing darker every minute.

"Hands, too," he added, holding them up for her inspection.

She smiled. "I'll bet you didn't drop a lot of footballs with those."

He took her hand and pretended to examine it. "Tiny. Like your feet."

"You're very critical tonight," she retorted.

"Me?" He gave her hand a gentle squeeze. "I think you are . . . just right."

She didn't know what to say to the unexpected compliment. They held hands and sat in darkness, watching lighted boats cruise into the bay to dock for the night.

Michael yawned. "Sorry. It's not the company."

"Don't apologize. It's been a long day for everyone," she said. "And thanks for taking care of the kids this afternoon. Barbara said you came over and picked them up."

"I was lonesome," he said simply.

Lonesome. How would he feel when he continued his trip? *Will he think about us?* she wondered. Her fingers felt the rough caress of his thumb as she reluctantly attempted to pull her hand from his. She pretended not to feel the warm shiver that rippled through her arm. "Well, good night, then."

He hooked his leg over hers to prevent her from getting off the chair. "Not yet."

She was stuck in an awkward position. His bare feet entwined with hers on the railing. "C'mon, Michael," she sputtered, "let me get up."

He chuckled. "I never knew when this old wrestling trick would come in handy." And then he added quietly, "Your legs felt like satin wrapped around me last night."

That soft comment weakened her. It shouldn't, she scolded herself, but it did. "Michael, about last night—"

"Shhh." His legs slid against hers as he tugged her closer to him, still holding the hand he had refused to let go. When he leaned forward to kiss her she welcomed the gentle pressure of his lips, unable to resist the deepening sensations rippling through her. With his free hand he cupped the back of her neck as the once-gentle kiss became more passionate and Allie, fears and objections whisked away as if by the mountain breezes, responded. His tongue played into her mouth, establishing a rhythm that pulled at Allie's senses while drumming heat through her body.

Michael had to touch her. What had started off as a way to keep her with him for a few moments longer had flared into a burning need to feel himself inside of her again. His hand left her neck to slide under her loose blouse and skimmed a path to her breasts, where her heart beat rapidly beneath warm skin. His fingers edged underneath lace to graze a tightened nipple and he felt Allie moan against his mouth.

Their lips played and caressed, nibbled and slid together enticingly once more. And when Michael slowly pulled away, Allie thought it seemed less a rejection and more a simple moment to recover from feelings stirred too intensely.

"I can't—" she began, regretting what she had to deny herself, especially when his hand slipped from underneath her blouse. But there were three children upstairs and no lock on her bedroom door. And she didn't want to fall in love.

Into the quiet Michael spoke. "I'll miss you tonight." He'd known he couldn't have her. Why had he thought he'd be content with kissing her? He took a deep breath. "Want to go running with me in the morning?"

"Sure," she breathed softly. "What time?"

He kissed her softly before answering, "Anytime. Whenever we're both awake."

She wondered if she would sleep at all tonight. "Okay."

He unwrapped his legs from around hers and stood beside her, still holding her hand. She scrambled to a sitting position, and he pulled her to her feet. "I have a feeling, sweet Alice," he murmured, kissing her hand gently before releasing it, "you're going to break my heart."

And before she could open her mouth to protest he was gone.

ALLIE WOKE EARLY MONDAY, dissatisfied after a restless night's sleep. But she was determined not to make any more mistakes; allowing herself to become serious about Michael would be her biggest one yet.

She met Michael in the kitchen, and to her relief, there seemed to be an unspoken agreement between them to keep things on a casual level. Lighthearted bantering continued throughout the morning, long after returning home from their run, past breakfast with the children. And later that morning, when Lydia called to offer a suddenly available cabin at the resort, Allie thanked her and refused. "Everything's fine the way it is," she told her.

"No, it's not!" called Danny, as Allie replaced the receiver and turned to see her son slumped into a kitchen chair. His sneakers were untied and the grass stains on his jeans were repeated on his face.

"What's wrong, Dan?" She walked over and sat down beside him. "Did you hurt yourself?"

He sighed, his eyes bleak as he looked up at her. "Nothing's fair."

And it's not written down anywhere that life has to be fair, Allie wanted to say. "Like what? What's not fair?"

"Why can't we be like everyone else?" he burst out.

"I didn't know we were different," she replied with a smile. What on earth was he getting at? Her older son with his thoughtful personality often hid questions or problems he thought would cause her worry or pain.

He looked almost apologetic. "We don't have a father and I think we should."

Allie thought about that for a moment. "Well, technically you do have one—"

"You know what I mean," he interrupted. "A *real* one, who lives with us. It doesn't count unless he lives with us."

Allie took a deep breath. "I understand what you're saying, Dan, but there isn't a whole lot I can do about it. If I could change it and make it different, I would." *I wouldn't have married the first boy who asked me, just to have a home of my own,* she thought. Her sons didn't know how lucky they were that Paul had fled to Alaska and decided to pretend his family never existed.

"Michael could stay." The heaviness of his words indicated the hopelessness he felt.

"Dan, you're old enough to understand that Michael is just a guest—a friend, now—but just because you want a father doesn't mean he could be one."

"I know." The child sighed. "But I thought I'd try it out. I've sort of pretended, y'know? I don't call him Dad or anything embarrassing like that, but I heard Glen call him that once, by mistake, I think. It gave me the idea."

Good heavens, what had Glen said to Michael? No wonder the man was ready to leave. He probably figured he'd made a mistake by taking a lonely woman to bed, because now he had a child calling him "Daddy," one pretending to, and Sherry hanging onto his knees every time he walked near her. How could she explain this to her son? "Dan, listen to me." When she thought she had his complete attention she continued, leaning forward across the table to brush the shaggy hair off his forehead. "Someday I hope I'll get married again, and he'll be a special person, a *very* special person who'll be an absolutely terrific father to all three of you kids."

Dan nodded. "Okay."

"But you can't make Michael that person, no matter how hard you try. He's not part of the family just because he's been staying with us. It doesn't work that way."

"But what about Sherry?" he protested. "*She's* part of the family."

Surprised, Allie didn't know what to say. She'd never fully explained Sherry to her sons, thinking they were too young to understand the sudden arrival of a ready-made sister. She hadn't realized Danny remembered much about that autumn. He had just started first grade and was in school most of the day. "True. But that's different," she argued lamely.

"But can I call Michael Dad in my head, just until he leaves?" He looked happy with the compromise.

"Don't you think that will make you miss him more when he goes away?" Where did she get this kid?

"Nah. But I think the little kids are gonna cry somethin' awful." He scraped back his chair, suddenly anxious to go back to the playhouse.

"Maybe. But we're a family—we'll stick together and help each other." Perhaps that did sound too much like *The Waltons*, she worried.

"Are you gonna cry too, Mom?"

She shook her head, fibbing to her son. There would most likely be some old-fashioned howling in the shower after Michael left. "Nope. I'm going to be glad we met Michael and had him as a friend for a while."

Dan looked dubiously at his mother. "Okay. I'm goin' out to help finish the playhouse. You want to see?"

"Sure. I'll be out in a minute." He raced back outside, the door slamming behind him. Allie propped up her chin with her hands and frowned. The children, so anxious for some male attention, had become too attached to Michael. Would his riding away on his bike cause mass hysteria? She didn't know how she was going to cope. The boys had been so young when their father left, and he hadn't hung around long enough to say goodbye. It had been late at night when he'd finished working a weekend shift at the restaurant, and he'd come home long enough to pick up clean clothes, all the cash in the house and hand her the keys to the truck. The waitress with him owned a new Jeep, or Allie figured Paul would have taken the truck, too. Some goodbye. Just a quick, "Sorry, Al, but I can't hack being tied down anymore. I'll write when I get settled somewhere and you can send the divorce papers."

She had stood frozen in shock, cold in her long flannel nightgown. To be honest, she had suspected something was wrong, but there hadn't been much time to dwell on the state of her marriage.

Allie stood up and gazed out the window at the children surrounding Michael in the playhouse. Too many memories. It wasn't fair. Danny was right. But there were no guarantees in life that said anything had to be fair. She'd learned that a long time ago.

"Knock, knock!" a voice called through the back door screen, interrupting Allie's thoughts.

She turned to see Jeanne. "Hi, come on in."

Her friend opened the door and handed her a bag of green beans. "I won't keep you. I just wanted to bring you some of the overload from my garden. With the wedding so close I don't have time to freeze or can any of it."

"This is terrific," Allie said, taking the heavy bag. "This is also dinner tonight. Come on in, have some iced tea with me."

"I don't want to interrupt anything," she said doubtfully, eyeing the vacuum cleaner in the middle of the kitchen floor. "I really wanted to know how you made out this weekend at the show."

Allie told her about the sales of the pictures, and the gallery interest as she fixed cold drinks. "All I have to do now is make some more pillows for the Huckleberry Festival."

"That's great, Al, but don't wear yourself out before the wedding. I worry about you."

Allie handed her friend her glass. "Why on earth would you worry about me?"

"You push yourself too hard. Raising three kids alone can't be easy." Jeanne leaned against the counter and continued, "Maybe I just want my friends to be as happy as I am now. I just wish you had someone, too."

"Maybe someday." She couldn't help glancing at the group at the playhouse. Michael was in the process of removing the hammer from Sherry's determined grip.

Jeanne watched the little scene along with her friend. "He's good with the children."

"Yes, he is."

"He seems, um, good with you, too."

"He is. We've had some fun together. Strange, I've only known him a short time, but I feel as if somehow he's been part of my life for a long time." Allie stopped, embarrassed to have said so much. She quickly drank her tea and looked away from the window.

"Maybe he'll stay," Jeanne offered quietly.

Allie met her gaze with a shrug. "Seems like everyone around here thinks he should. Everyone but Michael."

"Are you in love with him?"

Allie tried to laugh, but the sound rang hollow. "Would it make any difference?" She didn't want to love him. Sure, she was happy when he was with her, and making love with him had been like nothing she'd ever experienced before. But she didn't want to love him.

Jeanne looked at her closely, but didn't comment. "There's a wedding invitation for Michael in the green beans. Bob and I would like to have him join us, if he wants to. But if you don't feel comfortable about it, don't give him the invitation. I don't want to put you on the spot." She put her empty glass in the sink and gave Allie a quick hug. "Hang in there, Al. If Michael had wanted to leave before now he would have found a way."

Allie shook her head. "No, he's had to wait here for that new bike."

Jeanne pushed the door open and turned back to Allie. "Maybe. Maybe not. If you ask me, I think that man is exactly where he wants to be."

THE TALK at the post office Wednesday morning was about huckleberries. It was going to be a good year, according to one elderly man who supplemented his social security check by selling gallons of berries to a local restaurant.

"Any special area?" Allie asked Jim when she finished collecting her mail.

"Oh, you know the pickers." He shook his head. "They never tell what mountain or draw or wherever has berries. A serious huckleberry picker never reveals his secret spot."

Allie chuckled. "True," she agreed, grabbing Sherry's hand. She let the child carry the bundle of mail. "But I have my own places in mind, and maybe it's time to check them out."

"Well, they tell me the berries are comin' on early, so you'd better go get some before they're all gone." He gave her a wave as she left the building.

Allie thought about the mountains on the short drive up the hill to her home. A berry-picking expedition would be a good thing to do right now. Yesterday Michael had mentioned how much he'd like to get up into the mountains, and the kids were growing restless waiting for the kittens to be born. It was a cloudy day, but still warm—a good day for a hike.

Michael had a wrench in his hand and was hunched over Danny's bike when Allie guided the truck into the driveway.

He looked up and smiled as she and Sherry hopped out of the truck. "I thought I'd better raise the seat for Dan."

"Great," she replied, watching the skillful hands adjust a metal part on the bike frame she hadn't known existed. She swallowed, hard. Sherry, realizing Michael was too involved to pay any attention to her, scooted down the steps and over to the sandbox to see what Glen was doing there.

"Hey! Dan!" Michael's voice boomed good-naturedly as he looked around for the boy.

"Coming!" Dan ran up the steps, his face flushed.

"Try this. See how it feels." Michael held the old bicycle while Dan tested the seat's height.

"Hey, neat. Thanks."

"No problem." Michael looked pleased, and then puzzled to see Allie still standing nearby.

She cleared her throat. "Maybe you should show me what you just did, so I'll know next time this kid grows another few inches." She walked closer to them, still clutching her mail, and peered at the underside of the bike.

"Okay. Right here," Michael pointed. "You loosen this—" he mimed with the wrench "—then adjust this, then tighten what you loosened." He looked up at her patiently. "See?"

"Sure." She probably could have figured it out for herself, but it was nice to have someone show her the way it was done. "Thanks."

"He's going to need a bigger bike soon, though. Especially if he keeps growing so fast." He grinned at Dan. "But this will do for now. Go on, show me if it works."

"All *right*," shouted Dan as he took off down the road, showing off a little for Michael's benefit.

Michael put the wrench back in the garage and slid the wooden door shut. He looked pleased with himself, and Allie remembered Jeanne's comment about Michael being exactly where he wanted to be. For a moment she wondered if her friend might be right. And if she was, what did it mean? Allie tore her gaze away from the muscles rippling beneath Michael's green T-shirt and tried to remember what she had planned for the day.

"Huckleberries," she decided, speaking out loud.

"What?" He turned, absently wiping his palms on his denim shorts.

"I heard the huckleberries are starting, and it seems like a good day to go up the mountains and see. Would you like to do that?" Allie hoped he'd say yes. She wanted to show him the beauty of the woods. And the view of the lake from so high above Hope was a breathtaking sight she didn't want him to miss. There were so many things to share with him.

"Sounds good to me."

"Okay." She looked at his bare legs. "But you'd better wear long pants, and bring a long-sleeved shirt, too. We'll be in the brush." Her relief made her tone brusque.

"Yes, ma'am." He held out his hand, and she put hers into it, almost without thinking, and let him lead her down the steps to the house.

Later, after a hasty lunch and when plastic buckets had been collected and rinsed, Allie and Michael herded the children into the truck. Before she climbed in, Allie slid the garage door open, struggling slightly with the bulky contraption, and rummaged around inside the building until she found what she wanted: her chain saw.

"Why do you need that?" Michael called from the doorway. "Planning on cutting your own path to the berry bushes?"

"Very funny." She handed him the saw and went back into the garage for the can of gasoline. When she came out of the garage Michael backed out of her way, then helped her slide the heavy door shut. "Actually, I want to scout out firewood, and we might as well get some if we see any." She misinterpreted his frown, adding, "Don't worry, I have a Forest Service permit."

He carefully set the saw in the back of the truck, then took the gasoline can and arranged the empty berry buckets so they wouldn't tip over. "You actually use this thing?"

"Well, of course. You want me to chop down trees the old-fashioned way?"

He turned around and glared at her. "I don't want you doing it any way at all! That's a dangerous machine."

"You don't have to tell me that. I have it cleaned and serviced every year, and I'm careful when I use it." She concluded her statements with a self-righteous little nod toward the unsmiling man in front of her. She didn't tell him that she could barely lift the darn thing, but kept it for one of the neighbors she hired to cut up the logs she ordered from a local logger each fall. Michael's shocked reaction made her want to tease.

"If anyone turns on a chainsaw today, it's going to be me," he growled, waiting for an argument.

She just smiled sweetly. "Okay. Can we go now?"

He nodded, still frowning, and they were soon on their way. Allie drove silently. She knew she probably shouldn't have goaded him into looking so fierce, but it made sense to bring the saw. You never knew what trees could have fallen across the road, or even what easy firewood could be gathered. And any wood at all that she could bring home instead of buying helped out her budget. She pictured Michael cozily settled in the living room while the stove cracked and sizzled its comforting heat. He'd be sprawled on the couch on some wonderfully lazy November Sunday afternoon, newspapers strewn on the floor, while the kids played and a Seattle Seahawks football game roared from the television set. She quickly shook her head to dispel the tempting vision. She'd better watch herself, she thought, because daydreaming and driving up steep mountain roads did not go together. Instead she concentrated on turning onto the correct gravel road and they were soon jouncing toward the top of the mountain.

"Watch for bear and deer," Allie told the children, although the kids were making so much noise they would have run off any animal within five miles.

"Where are we?" Michael asked.

"Trestle Creek Road. We have a few miles to go." She glanced over to see Sherry nestled in Michael's lap, her eyes heavy with the need to doze off. The hard bouncing of the truck didn't seem to disturb her.

"Mom, I'm getting carsick," Danny whispered.

"Me, too," Glen groaned, and the boys giggled uncontrollably at their mother's concerned expression.

Danny patted his mother's arm. "It was a joke, honest, cross my heart! Pretty good, huh?"

"Oh, sure. That was great." Allie had to shift into a lower gear to negotiate the switchbacks in the steep road. She prayed she wouldn't meet any logging trucks. She could tell they were nearing the top when the trees thinned out, and a breeze swept through the truck's open windows. Rounding a turn, they were treated to a spectacular view of the lake. Michael whistled appreciatively.

"Not far now," she told him, pleased by his reaction to the sweeping views of mountainsides and blue water. The islands looked very small in the large expanse of lake. As the truck climbed higher, Allie's palms grew moist on the steering wheel. She carefully navigated the twists and turns, staying well away from the edge of the road. Finally they neared a large open area where the road ended. Allie parked the truck on a level spot beside some straggly brush. Michael gently nudged Sherry into waking while Allie let the boys clamber out of her side of the truck.

"Get the buckets," she told them before they could run off to explore. "And stay right here by me."

Sherry and Michael came around to the back of the truck. Michael reached into the truck bed and lifted the chain saw easily. He frowned once at Allie, as if afraid she might sneak back with some kind of awful desire to cut up logs when he wasn't looking. Allie thought his concern was very touching. If he only knew she had only operated that machine once, and the noise and imminent danger had terrified her so she hadn't started it up again.

"Let's lock the saw inside the truck, okay?" She smiled. "No use tempting anybody."

"Tempting who?" Michael asked wryly, surveying the empty area, devoid of people as far as he could see.

"Well, you never know who could come up here, it's not private property and the saw cost a lot of—"

"I was just teasing, Allie." He held up one hand as if to stop her flow of words. Sherry clung to his other hand as if afraid she would disappear if she didn't hang on to him.

The child looked questioningly at her mother. "Berries now?" She licked her tiny lips.

Allie handed her a small bucket. "Sure, sweetie. Let's go find some."

The boys raced around the truck, making enough racket to scare any self-respecting bear into the next county, which was fine with her. Bears and huckleberry patches just naturally went together, and many a picker had a story of "sharing" huckleberries with a hungry black bear.

"Which way?" Michael looked toward the top of the mountain.

"We'll angle off to the side, over there—" she pointed to a stand of trees "—and walk along through the brush. Berries grow on slopes, so you have to watch your step."

"Okay." He grinned. "You lead."

As they hiked, Allie kept an eye on the rambunctious boys. Now and then they passed empty bushes and the children groaned. "That's okay," Allie reassured them. "We'll find our spot soon."

"How did you learn about this?" Michael asked, crashing along behind her through the brush.

"Barbara took me up here last year. She's a relentless berry picker and makes all sorts of jam and pies and sauces. The kids ate as much as they picked last year so I didn't have as much to take home as I wanted, so we only got one batch of jam out of the expedition."

"And pancakes!" Glen cried. "Remember the pancakes?"

"Pick enough, and we'll have huckleberry pancakes for supper tonight."

They hiked on and were eventually rewarded with thickly laden berry bushes. Everyone scattered in different directions and began the tedious picking of the little purple berries. For a few moments all Allie could hear was the tiny plop of berries hitting the bottom of the plastic buckets. "Keep making noise," she called to the children, "so the bears can hear you."

Michael's large arms could reach farther than hers, and frequently he climbed higher on the slope to reach the bushes. Sherry stayed near Allie and ate more berries than she put into the bucket. The boys laughed with purple lips and held up stained fingers to show their mother.

"C'mon, you two! Save some for jam." She hoped they wouldn't make themselves sick.

Allie and Michael continued to pick berries throughout the afternoon, but the boys soon grew tired of the work and played army in an imaginary fort amid the rocks. Sherry wanted to be with them but the uneven footing bothered her; she could not figure out how to walk with one leg down hill and one leg up the hill, so she sat down in disgust to pick and eat whatever berries she could reach. It took more than two hours to fill two buckets, which was not bad considering the amount of berries consumed by the picking crew.

"Jam tomorrow," Allie announced with a satisfied sigh. She could feel the perspiration trickle down her back, and she wiped her damp forehead with the sleeve of her shirt. She carefully arranged the bucket on the uneven ground once more, and looked behind her to the lake. "And a swim this afternoon."

"Are you talking to me?" Michael called from the slope above her.

She raised her voice. "To myself, I guess. I think I'm finished."

"This was a great idea," he told her when he reached her. He carried a full bucket over to her.

"You've been eating the produce," she teased.

"How can you tell?" He laughed and Allie had to fight a sweeping desire to trace the outline of his lips with the tip of her tongue and taste the tartness of berries there.

"Your—lips are purple," she stammered.

"Well, yours aren't. Always the lady," he murmured thoughtfully. She didn't see his fingers pluck berries from the bucket until it was too late to back away. "Here," he said, setting the bucket on the ground before offering her the palmful of berries. "It's not fair, you know."

"What isn't?" She brushed leaves from his shirt. It was a good excuse to touch him.

"The rest of us are purple and you're not." He shook his head at her protest and fed the berries to her, one by one, her tongue sometimes slipping tantalizingly along the roughness of his finger, her lips occasionally caressing the callused thumb. His dark eyes looked into hers and his face lost its teasing expression and became serious.

Allie thought she would fall backward down the mountain and had to brace her sneakered feet against the rocky earth as Michael let the uneaten berries drop from his hand. He cupped her shoulders and dropped a light kiss on her lips.

"Mmm . . . juicy." He teasingly smacked his lips in satisfaction, but his low voice was husky. "Are we finished?" His twinkling eyes gave a different meaning to the question.

She laughed, happy to be with him. "I guess so."

He gently massaged her shoulders, then ran his hands lightly up the sides of her neck to tangle in her soft hair. "I'm going to have to get you all to myself again one of these days, Mrs. Leonard." His eyes crinkled at the corners as he smiled down at her. "Now that I've had you eating out of my hand, I have to take advantage—" He kissed her again, until Sherry tugged at his pant leg.

"Tiss me, too?" the child begged.

Allie and Michael laughed. The boys came running out of the bushes, sure they had heard a large animal nearby.

"Guess it's time to leave," Allie said reluctantly. She hated to have the afternoon end. She picked up the boys' forgotten buckets and her own full one.

Michael nodded his agreement and started back down the path. He held Sherry's hand and started to follow the boys.

"Michael! You forgot something!" she called after him.

He turned, surprised. "What?"

"Your berries." She held up her arms to show him she couldn't carry any more, and he and Sherry returned to her.

"Your fault," he murmured.

"Mine? How do you figure that?"

"You make me forget what I should be doing." He sighed. "But I'm getting used to it." He picked up the pail and smiled at her. "And I'm even beginning to like it."

"You are?" What happened to the man who kept pulling away from her, she wondered. She liked this side of Michael so much more.

"Yep. It was a nice afternoon. Thanks." He tugged Sherry's hand. "C'mon, babe, let's go back to the house and help your mom make those pancakes she promised."

Allie stood quietly for a moment before following the rest of the family back to the truck. She had scratches on her arms from plowing through the brush, her shirt stuck damply to her back and she was thirsty. But her heart soared. She licked the berry juice from her lips and remembered the taste of Michael's fingers.

9

THE GAILY DECORATED HOUSEBOAT creaked away from its wooden berth at the Bayside Marina, and the sun shone hot and bright upon the forty wedding guests assembled to celebrate with Jeanne and Bob. When the boat had cruised into the middle of the bay, Hope's mayor, a sturdy athletic woman with graying hair, read a simple but official rendition of the marriage ceremony.

Flowers dangled in clusters from the railings of the houseboat and crepe paper streamers fluttered in the breeze. Jeanne, roses in her hair and radiant in a pastel dress, recited her vows to her new husband. Allie, blinking back tears, thought it was the most beautiful wedding she'd ever seen.

Michael grasped her hand and she clung to it. A warm feeling snaked up her arm and circled her chest in a heated warmth that had nothing to do with the sunshine reflecting off the boat's painted deck.

He bent to whisper, "This is my favorite part."

She blinked, forcing herself out of her reverie to listen. "What?"

"The happy ending."

She watched as Jeanne and Bob kissed, then turned to smile happily at the crowd. Congratulations burst from everyone as the guitarist picked a jubilant melody from her instrument. Michael pulled Allie into the line of people waiting to congratulate the bride and groom.

"You believe in such things?" she asked in surprise.

"Sure." He squeezed her hand, smiling down into her eyes. "Don't you?"

"Not from personal experience, no." She shrugged. "Besides, my wedding was nothing like this."

He grimaced. "Neither was mine. A brief ceremony at city hall, after school one Friday afternoon."

She couldn't believe he was actually talking about it, and so openly, too. "Mine was worse," she countered lightly. "A tacky wedding chapel about sixty miles from here, famous for its ask-no-questions weddings. I was only eighteen, but I felt so grown-up."

They edged closer to Jeanne and Bob, but the line moved slowly.

"How long have you been divorced?"

She was surprised he'd never asked her that before. "Almost four years now. Sometimes it seems like more than that. Other times I wonder how the time has gone by so quickly. Why are you frowning?" He looked fierce all of a sudden.

Four years? Strange—he'd always assumed it had been recent. He did some rapid mental arithmetic. "This is none of my business," he growled, "but who wanted the divorce?"

"He did. There was another woman—"

"But Sherry must have been a baby, or were you pregnant? What kind of man would walk out on his family?" Michael knew with cool certainty how good it would feel to use Paul Leonard as a tackle dummy.

"It wasn't like that. Please, would you keep your voice down?" She was afraid they were attracting attention, and she had no intention of explaining that part of her life. "Maybe it's bad luck to talk about divorces at a wedding."

Moments later she stood in front of Jeanne and Bob. Michael dropped her hand in order to shake hands with the groom, and the two men exchanged words quietly while Allie and Jeanne hugged. Then Michael kissed Jeanne's cheek. She whispered something that made him chuckle and shake his head before following Allie inside.

"I volunteered to serve champagne," she told him.

He nodded, and started to help her without asking. He made so many trips outside to pop the corks from the bottles Allie soon lost count. She kept pouring while others served, and soon Bob was toasting his bride. The laughing couple were the recipient of many toasts, both serious and funny, as the houseboat, engines vibrating under the wooden deck, made its way past the point that marked the entrance to the bay and toward the small islands.

Michael wandered over to the boat's railing as they entered the main body of the lake. Allie thought, for the seven- or eight-hundredth time, how handsome he looked. His beige slacks and brown-checked shirt emphasized his dark good looks. She couldn't keep her eyes off him, and caught herself watching him when she should have been picking up empty plastic glasses.

He can't know how I feel about him. How pathetic she felt. She'd fallen for the first guy who'd ridden through town. She smiled to herself, thinking of the old Westerns with the lone cowboy who stops at the widow's ranch. At the end he always rode off into the sunset—alone—as the brave woman, waving goodbye, stood on the rickety porch. The eighties version wasn't much different, she mused. Except she didn't have a bonnet. Just a new white sundress, and she'd left her straw hat on the kitchen table.

"You look as if you're up to some mischief." Michael smiled, approaching her. "I think that's when you and Glen look alike."

"I've been told that before," she hedged.

He touched her hair, admiring its red highlights in the sun. "Pretty color. The boys have it, too. Sherry must look like her father." He hadn't been able to get their earlier conversation out of his mind. He wondered if the man had ever seen the child. Probably not, if he had left before she was born.

She frowned. "Yes." She hesitated, reluctant to say anything more. She'd been Sherry's mother for so long it was hard to remember that she hadn't given birth to the child. But this wasn't the right time to explain that to the handsome teasing man in front of her. "Want to know something?" At his nod, she continued, happy to change the subject. "I've been wondering how you'd look in a cowboy hat."

"Sorry. I don't own one." His dark eyes twinkled. "Will my orange helmet do?"

"Perfectly." His arm circled her bare shoulders in a casual embrace. She had to remind herself how casual it was as she ducked quickly away from him. "See you later. I'm off to serve wedding cake."

Allie was glad she had something else to do besides stare at Michael like some lovesick teenager. Inside the roomy cabin of the houseboat, she managed to avoid him for the next hour. She caught a glimpse of him when Jeanne and Bob cut the cake, and then she was busy slicing the remainder for the guests, most of whom were friends and neighbors. She served the last piece of frosted cake onto a little paper plate. Finished, she was about to lick the frosting off her fingers when her hand was grabbed.

Michael pulled it to his lips and licked her thumb. "That's mine."

She slipped her hand from his, hastily wiping her trembling fingers on a napkin. Didn't he know how he affected her? Embarrassed, she handed him a plate.

"Thanks." He set the cake back on the table. "Do you want to swim? I think they're going to stop the boat for a while."

"You go ahead. I'll catch up in a little while."

He looked uncertain, but left the room, his broad back and shoulders filling the narrow doorway.

Barbara, holding a large garbage bag away from her crimson jumpsuit, approached the table. "What are you doing?" she asked, noting Allie's expression.

"Practicing." She sighed, turning back to wipe the frosting off the silver knife.

"For what?"

She looked up at the empty doorway. "Practicing watching that man walk away."

"Oh." Barbara scooped used paper plates and napkins into the bag. "How bad is it?"

"I'll live," she said lightly, unwilling to reveal any more of her feelings. "Thanks again for having the kids at your house today. I told Tina I'd pay her extra because they were spending the night."

"No problem. They all get along so well, and Tina can handle them."

"Go change," Jeanne ordered, coming into the cabin. "You two are making me feel guilty. All you've done is work."

"Did I tell you how much I love your dress?" Allie asked.

"Yep." She tried to fan herself with a napkin. "But it's hot and I can't wait to go swimming. Let's go."

Barbara offered, "I think Allie's hiding."

"Why? Michael's been wandering around looking lost. I think Bob and Ron have introduced him to everyone here at least twice." Jeanne frowned at Allie.

"I noticed. He's been the center of attention for the past hour."

"Well, go center his attention on you," Barbara ordered.

"You know, Allie," Jeanne added, "maybe you're keeping him at a distance when he doesn't want to be that far away."

Allie shook her head. "When his bike comes, he'll be gone. It's that simple, and my feelings aren't going to make any difference."

"Wrong. What if—this is just a thought, mind you—what if our friend Michael knew someone who worked for the United Parcel Service?"

"Bob?" Allie shot a confused look to Barbara. "What's she getting at?"

Barbara shrugged, and Jeanne continued, "And what if your friend told the delivery person right in his neighborhood to deliver any packages to him at this friend's house, not the place where he was staying. And suppose a certain method of transportation had been sitting neatly boxed, under an old blanket, in someone's garage for three whole days?"

Allie was stunned. Jeanne could only mean Michael's new bike had arrived. But he hadn't told her. He hadn't left.

Barbara asked eagerly, "How did you find out?"

Jeanne lowered her voice as more people filtered into the room. "I was moving my things into Bob's house and boxing up stuff we had duplicates of, for a garage sale. I found the bike by accident. Then I asked Bob about it and found out why he had it."

"Why didn't you tell me sooner?" Allie cried.

"Give me a break," Jeanne said, laughing, "I've been busy getting married."

Allie gave her a hug. "Thanks. I'm going to change. Then I'm going to ask Michael why he hid his bike." But she thought she already knew the answer and wondered what last Saturday night had to do with it.

"Don't do that," Barbara groaned.

"And if you do, don't say I told you," Jeanne added.

"Okay, okay. I'll see you later." She left the cabin to pick up the beach bag she'd stored under an outside bench. Her thoughts whirled. She couldn't figure out why Michael hadn't told her about his bike. What did it mean? If he'd wanted to stay and go to the wedding he could have just said so. Surely he knew he could stay camped in the yard for a few more days. For the rest of his life, actually.

No, she thought, frowning. He probably didn't know that. She must have given him the impression she wanted him to leave. How could she confront him about his bike? Could she find out his feelings without exposing her own?

When it was her turn in the tiny bathroom she locked the door and swiftly changed into her bathing suit. Moments later, when she went outside, she saw Michael. Dark and handsome in his navy-blue trunks, one of her best bath towels thrown over his shoulders, he stood watching the crowd of swimmers in the water.

She walked to him, still wondering what she would say. "Hi."

"Hi yourself." He smiled down at her. "I've been trying to remember where we went fishing. Are we near there?"

She pointed south, past the islands close by. "No, we're still a few miles away."

"I wish I could go back before I leave, but there won't be time."

She fought the tightening in her throat. "When are you leaving?"

"Tomorrow."

Tomorrow. The word, in its devastating simplicity, took a few seconds to sink in. "What about your bike?" She couldn't look at him, turning instead to the stunning view of darkly etched mountaintops and turquoise sky. It hurt her eyes.

"It arrived a few days ago. Bob kept it in his garage for me."

"Why didn't you tell me?" She hoped her voice sounded normal.

He touched her shoulder, forcing Allie to look at him. "I would have had to leave sooner—and I wanted to come to the wedding, to be with you today. Besides," he admitted, "I wanted to make love to you again. And again. I needed the excuse to stay longer."

She looked into those warm brown eyes. "You didn't need any excuse," she whispered. It had been a very long week.

"I thought I did." He took her hand. "How long is this boat trip?"

"Until five."

"Do you have any plans for the evening?"

She shook her head. "Not until now."

"Good. How's dinner sound?"

"Like a very good idea." She would have the evening with him. She'd have to be grateful for that much.

"Okay, Mrs. Leonard, it's a date. I hope I can wait that long. Are you ready to go swimming?"

"Uh . . ." She hesitated. Beaches were one thing, open water something entirely different. "I don't know if I can tread water very long."

"I'll rescue you if you start to go under."

"Oh, really?" She didn't like the thought of going under, either.

He grinned. "I'm very good at mouth-to-mouth resuscitation."

"Hmm..." She pretended to think it over. She enjoyed this side of him, the gentle teasing and sense of humor that made her feel as if she'd known him all her life. "I guess I'll have to depend on that, then."

He took her hand and led her to the open gate near the bow of the boat. "Jump."

"Don't look. I have to hold my nose."

"You're kidding." He stopped, poised on the edge.

She laughed. "Nope. You go first."

"Not on your life. You'll disappear and I'll have to swim all alone." He grabbed her, tugging her into the water with him as he jumped. She barely had time to grab her nose before splashing into the icy coldness of the lake. It was a shock after the warm water of the campground's shallow bay. She trod water and flipped the hair out of her eyes with one hand.

"Hey, you're alive." Michael bobbed to the surface and shook his head, smoothing the thick hair from his forehead. He swam closer. "You're gasping for air, though. Can I help you?"

"That mouth-to-mouth stuff again? That line is pretty old," she retorted, pleased by the look of warmth on his face.

"So am I," he sputtered. "Pretty old, I mean."

"Oh, I don't think so."

"Are you saying I'm a man of experience?" he teased, his face just inches away from hers.

"I have no idea," she said with a laugh. "I haven't experienced you...for days." The risqué words tumbled out, surprising Allie with her own boldness.

"If that's an invitation, I accept." He tucked one dripping strand of hair behind her ear and let his fingers trail to the top of one breast. "Swim to the island?"

She assessed the short distance warily. "I don't know if I can make it that far." She knew she would drown if he kept touching her like that though.

"I'll be with you all the way. We can't just keep on treading water."

"We could get back on the boat," she suggested, knowing that was not at all what he had in mind.

"And lose you in the crowd again? No way," he whispered in her ear.

It was against her better judgment. "Okay. I'll try." What could happen on an island, with all these people around? Nothing. She started the long strokes to the beach. Was that good or bad? Michael wanted to be alone with her. He had made that obvious, and she liked it. Did it mean he cared? She tried to focus her attention on her meager swimming ability. She could feel him beside her, feel the little ripples of water as he swam near.

She paced her breathing, slowing down her strokes. Maybe the island wasn't as close as it looked. She could see the rocks at the bottom of the clear water.

"We're almost there," he said. "You'll be able to touch bottom pretty soon."

She tried. "Not yet." She flipped onto her back and kicked her way in to shore until his shout kept her from running headfirst into a log. She stopped and stood on the rocky bottom in waist-high water.

She hadn't been on the island since last summer. The tiny curved bay was shadowed by fir trees. It was a small island, privately owned. The No Trespassing sign tacked to a dying tree was faded and worn, and there were signs of an old camp fire along the shore.

Michael stood on the beach, his hands on his hips, a grin on his face. "This is fantastic."

"You look like the king of the mountain," she panted.

"I feel like Robinson Crusoe," he announced, and started to explore beyond the tree line.

"Hey! Wait a minute!" she called. She heard the noise of the swimmers and music coming from the houseboat, but she didn't know how long it would anchor nearby. "We don't want to get left behind!"

She looked back at the boat again, shading her eyes with her hand. Light glinted off binoculars, as someone in red, probably Barbara, looked toward the island. Allie waved, wanting whoever it was to know where they were, and the figure waved back. Allie felt a little better and turned toward the woods to find Michael.

There was the small path she remembered, having come here once with the Cub Scouts. Not a relaxing experience, she remembered, but one they'd needed for their water badges. She followed the path, calling, "Michael!"

"Over here," he answered, and she brushed back overhanging branches to emerge onto another open area. He stood on a skinny finger of land that pointed to Hope. The town sat peacefully on its edge of the mountain, while cars could be seen zipping along the highway near the lake. The beach was white with smooth rocks.

"This was a favorite summer camping area for Indians," she said. "I heard they used to look for flint for their hunting weapons on this island." She walked closer to him, enjoying the view of the lake and the town sheltered above it. "Can you see my house? The shiny roof to the left of the big fir trees?"

It took him a moment, but then he nodded.

Allie sat down on the beach. "There could be arrowheads in here." She began to sift carefully through the rocks. "Sometimes you can find partial ones—something they made that just didn't work out."

"Here," he said, coming over to sit close beside her. "I'll help you look."

"We can't stay long," she cautioned. "The boat's on the other side of the island and we don't want them to leave without us."

He smiled. "You mean," he asked in mock horror, "we'd have to spend the rest of our lives on a deserted island together?"

"I don't think Tina would want to baby-sit that long," she countered dryly. "Besides, since you're leaving tomorrow, don't you need to get home to pack?" She said it to remind herself as well as Michael. She hated the thought of his leaving. Why did he have to go? But, she told herself for the millionth time, he is temporary. And she didn't need temporary—she needed permanent.

He sighed. "Yes. I do."

She watched as he lay back on the smooth beach. He closed his eyes, as if thinking. She didn't want to disturb him, lost in her own thoughts about the wedding. What a lovely ceremony it had been. Those words of love, those promises, had touched her deeply. Could she say them again, after rejecting those vows the first time? Would she want to? She wanted the man beside her, and her heart gave the answer. Oh, yes, she could. She could make the promise to love, honor and cherish with confidence, as much confidence as anyone could have about the future. He was a special man.

But he wasn't hers.

She looked back across the water to Hope. A lot of things had happened to her in that tiny community. She had friends, children, a life with work she was proud to do. If loneliness was her only problem—well, she was lucky. *Face it, Allie, you're going to be a lot lonelier after tomorrow.*

"An arrowhead for your thoughts," Michael offered, his voice quiet and serious. He sat up and looked at her closely.

"Nothing important. Just daydreaming." Her lips curved into a gentle smile. "Besides, you haven't found one."

"I'll start looking if you'll talk to me."

She shook her head. "We'd better go."

He stood, helping her up. "Okay."

She started back the way they had come, through the wooded path, when he called her back.

"Let's walk around the island. It can't be that big," he suggested, holding out his hand.

She clasped his hand, still cool from the lake water, but strong and secure as he led her around a huge driftwood pile and on to the side of the island that faced the open water. Fishermen in various-sized boats trolled in the distance, and a speedboat trailing a water skier roared past.

Michael and Allie followed a tiny path under some trees to the top of a rocky cliff that jutted out into the shadowy green darkness on the lake. A curious bee buzzed around them before disappearing in the woods. The heat and quiet were part of the island, and neither Michael nor Allie wanted to break the spell of the island silence.

Michael stopped suddenly as a black garter snake wiggled across their path. "I almost stepped on him."

Allie froze until the snake slithered into the brush. "Ugh. In bare feet?"

He chuckled. "Be careful where you step. I think we have to walk through the woods to get back to the cove."

When they came out on the other side, to the tiny beach where they had started from, Allie felt sorry their walk had been so short. She pulled away from his hand, preparing to swim back to the houseboat, selfishly wishing she could have had more time alone with him. She was shocked to discover she could have all the time she wanted. "They're leaving without us," she cried.

"I see that," he answered calmly. Too calmly.

Allie made a futile attempt to get the boat's attention by jumping up and down on the beach, waving furiously and calling for Jeanne.

"I don't think they can hear you." Laughter coated his words.

"This is not funny," she grumbled, turning to frown at him. He didn't seem particularly concerned. Her eyes narrowed. "Did you *plan* this?"

He held up one hand, taking a step backward. "I had nothing to do with it. Honest."

Allie remembered waving to the figure in red. Had Barbara interpreted that as a signal to leave without them? "Did Barbara drink enough champagne to tell the story of Tina being conceived on this island?"

He laughed. "Yes. I told her I thought that was terrific. Ron said he'd told her they were going fishing. But Barbara wouldn't have set this up."

"You don't know her like I do. Give her an idea like that and she'll organize it. Especially—"

"Especially what?"

Especially when she has such a romantic soul, Allie thought. But she didn't say anything. She trusted Barbara to get them off the island eventually, and the children were safe with Tina. They were even going to spend the night at the Millers's house since the wedding reception was going to continue on land, at a local bar with a country and western band to dance to. "Nothing. I still can't believe this. It must be her idea of a joke."

"Probably. If not, someone will realize we're not on the boat and come back for us."

"They couldn't possibly leave us here with no blankets or food—it gets cold at night." She tried to sound convincing. Maybe she'd believe it.

"They'll be back to pick us up later, I'll bet. C'mon, haven't you always wondered what it would be like to be stuck on a deserted island?" He touched her shoulder, a comforting gesture that ended as a caress. When she turned to him he bent to kiss her lightly. "There."

"Is that supposed to make me feel better?" His bare chest was definitely distracting her.

"Yes," he insisted, "I want you to feel happy to be alone with me. I want you to feel the way I do."

"And how's that?" It was a tempting question to ask. She couldn't wait, she decided as she gazed up into his warm dark eyes, to hear the answer.

"Like this," he murmured, and kissed her in a way that made her heart stop for a second in surprise, then pound rapidly as if to make up the time lost. *Make up for time lost.* Her body urged her to do just that. It would be so easy to slip into his arms. After all, there was little material between them. Her rose maillot slid silkily against his furry chest, tempting her further as the kiss deepened.

It was different from the last time he'd held her, and yet familiar in that passion welled so easily between them— passion she'd tried to control all week. She'd erected barriers between them and she didn't even know why anymore.

Allie returned the kiss with the feelings she'd been saving in her heart and body. She loved this man, and there could be no turning back. This time he couldn't leave her and walk away. The island wasn't big enough. She reached gently to touch his shoulders, feeling the smooth skin with its sunlit warmth beneath her fingertips. Almost without conscious thought, she lifted her lips to his once more and accepted without hesitation the force of his kiss.

It was so right. As their lips separated reluctantly, she opened her eyes to look at Michael. He held her closer to him while she rested her head against his solid chest, inhaling the fresh sunshine smell, enjoying the unrestricted exploration her fingers made along his back, stroking, feeling. It was too good to be true, she decided, having this feeling again, with all the time in the world to enjoy it.

"Allie," he sighed into her hair.

She waited, unmoving, for him to step away. But he held her tightly, his arms wrapped snugly around her back. "What?"

"You are so special to me."

Words. What power they had over people, she mused. Special, special . . . a lovely echo. "No one's coming for us right away, are they?"

"No," he whispered, his arms tightening around her.

Allie wanted to believe it. She could hold him for the rest of the day. And night. That was an intriguing thought. But she didn't want to spend any more time thinking.

He broke away, and tugged her hand gently. "Let's get out of the sun," he said huskily. He led her to a shaded area, behind the budding huckleberry bushes, where soft pine needles made a scented carpet as if waiting for lovers. He kissed her again, and her toes sank in the soft needles under her feet.

All thoughts ceased as Michael's large hands skimmed over the material that enveloped her slim body, sliding slowly down to the dip of her waist. Her stomach fluttered in anticipation as he held her, his fingers making their tingling warmth-giving journey along her body. He cupped one breast gently, as his fingertips slid enticingly along the bathing suit's bodice. Allie suddenly ached to be out of it, but wanted to make sure, needed to know if this was really happening. She ran her hands along his chest, to let him know how much she wanted him. He groaned into her open mouth, his tongue swirling temptingly in delightful patterns. Allie strained against him, eagerly welcoming the force of his hard body. She had to have him once more before he left.

From somewhere above them an angry bird cawed its complaints. Michael pulled away from Allie slowly, and smiled down into her glowing face. "I feel like a kid with his first girl."

"This does seem sort of...secret, doesn't it?" She glanced around the shaded woods, then back to the man in front of her. The fierce longing in his eyes echoed her own. As if in answer, she stepped backward, tugged at the bodice of her bathing suit and stripped it off in a fluid motion.

He drew in his breath. "You're beautiful."

"Your turn," she insisted softly, tossing the slip of fabric to one side.

They sank onto the soft ground, Michael stroking luxurious patterns over Allie's heated skin. She closed her eyes, feeling her bones melt into liquid fire as his lips sought her breasts and continued their burning journey along her abdomen and downward. He knelt over her, his fingers tenderly parting intimate feminine folds, dipping into the moist center of heat.

"So sweet," he whispered against her thighs as she relaxed into his touch. His lips sought to bring pleasure, until minutes later Allie trembled with the effort it took to control her response.

"Not...this...way," she gasped.

"How, then?" His voice was husky with passion as he slid alongside her.

"Together," she murmured, reaching for him. "Now." She wanted him inside her, wanted the release to come when they were joined. Her small hand pulled at the elastic of his swim trunks and delved inside to release the satin length of him.

"I thought you'd never ask." Michael drew off his trunks and kicked them aside. He lay above Allie, supporting his weight with his arms, and smiled down at her, dropping a light kiss on her mouth as his body covered hers.

His eyes darkened with her answering smile.

Her hands stroked his bare back and she murmured huskily, "I've missed the feel of you," while her fingertips urged him closer. He entered her slowly, a silky smooth motion that left her straining for more.

He filled her then, and she gasped with sharp pleasure and began to move with him. Together they gave to each other, over and over again, until spiraling tremors burst through her body. He strengthened his thrusts, prolonging the intensity of her release, then moaned her name as he shuddered deeply inside her.

She caressed his muscled shoulders, smoothed her trembling hands along his back, while he nibbled kisses against the satiny warmth of her neck. Allie was barely aware of the fragrant scent of pine, the muffled lap of tiny waves washing up on the beach, the whisper of a breeze near the top of the trees. "Oh, Michael," she murmured sadly into the damp curls of hair around his ear, "this is a hell of a way to say goodbye."

"THANKS, EVERYBODY!" Allie called, making her way down the plank that connected the houseboat to the marina's splintered dock. She had already thanked Jeanne and Bob for their hospitality, scolded a too-angelic Barbara and fended off the many humorous comments by other guests ever since the boat had returned to the island on its journey back to the bay. "This will be all over town by tomorrow," she muttered to Michael, who didn't seem the least bit concerned.

"So? We were stranded on an island. Perfectly innocent, if you ask me." His weight bounced the plank as he walked behind her.

Her body weakened when she remembered how perfectly *un*innocent the past hours had been. The only other man who had ever been in her life, Paul, had never made her feel like that before. "Nobody will ask *you* anything because you won't be around." *Tell me you're not going,* she invited silently. *Tell me.*

"Allie . . ." Michael hesitated, taking her elbow as they reached the dock.

She tugged her arm away. "Please don't make a scene."

They followed other departing guests to the parking lot and, amid waves and goodbyes, crossed the highway to the road that led up the hill to home. It was a steep walk, and they didn't speak. Allie was tired, her efforts concentrated on making it to the house without falling flat on her face in the street.

"We need to talk," he began, as they entered the yard.

She resisted the urge to lean into his strength, squaring her shoulders and moving farther away from him. "I know." She opened the kitchen door and Michael followed her into the empty house.

"The kids are all at Barbara's for the night?"

"Yep." She went to the sink, pouring herself a glass of cold water and drinking thirstily. "Want some?"

"And what about us?" He leaned easily against the counter, facing her.

"Us?"

"I'm going to take you upstairs and make love to you again. In a soft bed, this time."

"Are you complaining about pine needles?" She experienced the familiar tingle again at the thought of their bodies entwined together. She had no regrets, but to have it happen again, when she was certain he wouldn't stay with her, would be like standing in the middle of the railroad tracks waiting for a train to mow her down.

He seemed to understand what she was feeling. He opened his arms wide, beckoning to her. She slipped inside of them easily. He was right for her, he was wrong for her. Stay or go—he would know he was loved.

"Don't leave," she whispered into the crumpled fabric of his shirt.

"I have to." His voice was ragged with pain, and she sensed the mysteries surfacing again.

Her arms tightened around him, holding him closer. "I'm so angry with you," she murmured.

His apology was a kiss, and Allie clung to Michael until they climbed hand in hand up the stairs to her room.

MUCH LATER, when twilight washed the bedroom with a dusky pink light, Allie lay in Michael's arms. Sadness threatened to overwhelm her as she said, "We're running out of time."

He didn't pretend to misunderstand. "I know."

"You're leaving—when?"

"First thing in the morning."

She forced herself to shove aside her independence and admit her need and love for this man. She rubbed one hand lazily around his chest as she lay in the crook of his arm. "Stay with me, please. I—I love you."

His arms tightened around her, and he shifted to his side to face her, his dark eyes shadowed. "I can't. Not now."

"You've said that before. And I never have understood."

He released her and slid to a sitting position, ready to leave. With her eyes she traced the ridge of backbone under his skin, and she resisted the urge to stroke one fingertip down its length.

"I told you once before I didn't have a lot to give you." He looked down at his hands, and then he got off the bed and pulled on his slacks.

"I didn't believe you then. And I still don't." She covered herself with part of the sheet within grabbing distance.

"I didn't tell you anything about my wife," he said bitterly. "She was a woman with a lot of problems I didn't know about."

"Oh, Michael—"

He held up his hand. "Wait a minute. Hear me out," he cautioned. "I thought I loved her, but I couldn't give her what she needed. She just didn't seem to care." He sat heavily on the edge of the bed. "I don't know why she married me. She hated being pregnant with our child, and shortly after the baby was born she moved out."

Allie's heart went out to him. She had always known there was more for him to tell. "What about your...child?"

He was grim, his lips white and set. "She left the baby with me, and I spent the summer taking care of her. The divorce was fast, but before the judge could award final custody to me, my *wife*—" he spat the word "—took my daughter and disappeared."

"Oh, Michael," she whispered, with tears in her eyes. She could feel the pain that radiated from him. She wondered if he would let her touch him, and sat up to lean toward him. When she held out her hand he took it, grasping as if hanging on for life. She had to ask. "What happened?"

"I never saw them again. They were killed in a car accident east of here, in Montana."

His flat words twisted her heart, while somewhere in her brain a warning sounded. "I thought you said your daughter drowned," she said gently, wondering why it mattered. But somehow it did.

"Technically." He nodded. "They never found a trace of Kate—my daughter," he explained in a low voice. "The local authorities did their best, but I guess deaths in rivers and lakes are no surprise to people around here. When they contacted me in Oregon about the accident and learned there was an infant . . . Well, there was no hope."

Allie knew that happened. Sometimes bodies were lost forever. "Have they . . . found her now? Is that why you need to go?"

"No." He sighed, dropping her hand. "Are you sure you want to hear all this?"

"Come here," she commanded gently as she placed pillows beside her against the headboard. He came to the side of the bed and lay beside her. "Better?"

"Yes. Much." His smile was twisted. "You're good for me."

It was the other way around, she knew. But he wouldn't believe her. "Now, tell me the whole story."

"Last winter a man—Will Wentworth, from Libby—wrote to me. He was a sheriff then, and on a fishing trip to Canada the night of the accident. He'd remembered seeing a woman eating alone in a small café in Troy—a town near the Montana-Idaho border—where he'd stopped for sandwiches. He even remembered an old van in the parking lot. Later, when he returned home, he heard about the accident and thought it was strange he hadn't seen a baby with her in the café."

"Couldn't she have left her in the van, asleep?" It wasn't a wise thing to do, but Allie knew people did it.

"That's what I thought, too, but Will didn't think so. He even talked to the waitress, who said the woman was there for almost three hours, like she was waiting for someone. And she never went outside to check on a child. Will believes Kate was not in the van when it went over the bridge."

"Bridge?" she repeated numbly. The warning bell grew louder. Allie knew this information was familiar. There were too many coincidences here. If she could just think for a minute...

But Michael continued. "I buried my wife in Oregon and threw myself in my work—the sports shop, the students, coaching. I thought I'd forgotten—until Will's letter. And even then, I picked the slowest way possible." He laughed grimly. "My bike. I think I was almost grateful when your kids ran over it. I realized it delayed a trip I didn't want to take. Even though it's been years."

"Years? Why didn't that man contact you before this winter?"

"He'd had a heart attack, lots of health problems, and retired early. He spends his winters in Arizona now. But he had traced the van to a traveling family who sell wilderness-type cookbooks."

"The Montana cookbook people?" She remembered she'd never given Michael the message, hadn't even thought about it until this minute.

"How'd you know that?" He looked at her in surprise.

She frowned. "I'm sorry. I forgot. The man—Joe? Came up to me at the craft show and told me to tell you he was sorry he couldn't help you."

He nodded. "It doesn't matter. I knew that already. He told me there was no child with Kathy when he traded his van for her car. But I don't hold out much hope that Katie's alive somewhere. That's pretty farfetched."

"Kathy?" The earth was spinning. Allie could feel its dizzy motion.

"My wife. I knew what kind of woman she was, but I didn't know what she was capable of doing to my life."

Or to mine, thought Allie, as the earth settled with a sickening thump, like an old elevator. The bedroom seemed very far away, as if she was sinking into a tunnel.

"I've lived with the guilt," she heard him say, "knowing if I'd taken better care of my daughter she'd be alive now. I didn't protect her the way I should have and I lost her. To not know if she's dead or alive or whatever happened to her—it's been hell." He touched Allie's shoulder, gliding his hand down her arm comfortingly. "You're very pale. I'm sorry I've upset you. But now you know why I have to go, don't you?"

She cleared her throat, trying to erase the lump there. "When did your wife leave?"

"Almost three years ago. Katie was three months old."

"She'd be—Sherry's age now." The words tried to choke her.

"Don't you think I haven't thought of that?" He flung himself restlessly from the bed and went to stand in front of the window. "Don't you think every time I see a little girl I wonder what my daughter would have looked like? The first time I saw Sherry I thought of Kate." He smiled at Allie. "Maybe that's why staying here became so important to me."

"Tell me about—about Katie." Maybe she was wrong, maybe this was just some dreadful coincidence that had no connection with her life. Some simple words from Michael could put her world back into place again.

He looked out the window at the lake, watching the sun drop below the western mountains. "We named her Katherine Michelle. Kathy wanted Michelle for her first name but I wanted a little replica of her mother. Crazy, isn't it? She had black hair, little wisps of fluff that stuck out all over her head. And the smallest toes . . .

"She was a beautiful child," he continued softly, "but Kathy didn't seem very attached to her. I never understood why she took her away from me, unless it was for revenge. She'd accused me of loving the child more than I did her—and it was the truth."

"You must have loved her once, or you wouldn't have married her," she offered.

He shook his head. "I think I loved the idea of helping her. She was so beautiful. . . ." He turned away from the window and faced Allie. "I was out of my league from the very beginning." He shoved his hands into his pockets, awkward now that Allie knew his story. "I think I'd better sleep in the tent tonight."

"You don't have to," she told him, but she knew what his answer would be. He needed the time alone, she guessed, and so did she. He had supplied her with the rest of the puzzle pieces, and now she had to assemble the picture and make some sense from it.

"Yes," Michael said wearily, coming to kiss her lightly on the forehead. "I do." He couldn't bear to see the pity in her eyes, no matter how hard she was trying to hide it. He left her then, and wondered to himself if he had done the right thing by telling her so much.

He walked out to the backyard and took great gulps of the cool night air. It would be simple to stay here, wrapped up in one of Allie's quilts, enjoying the rest of the summer with a woman who seemed to understand him. It would be easy to keep on pretending to be one big happy family, but he was tired of pretending. He had to leave, and telling Allie why had been a step in the right direction.

ALLIE LISTENED to the back door close before she slumped against the pillows. Her head ached from too much sun, her body was weighted with exhaustion. But her mind wouldn't stop questioning. She wasn't sure what was happening, wanting only to deny any knowledge that would require a decision. How could it be the same child? How could it not be?

It was before she had moved to Hope, before a real estate agent offered her a staggering amount of money for the log cabin and riverfront property she and Paul had purchased years before the area had been discovered by tourists. She remembered a cool October day, the kind of weather that gave people energy to ready themselves for winter. Kathy had appeared, surprising her old friend by arriving in the driveway in a dusty foreign car. The small baby she had with her was cranky, obviously tired and needing a bath.

"How did you find me?" Allie asked her, wondering why Kathy had made the effort. Their teenage friendship in the same foster home had slowly dwindled over the past ten years. Allie had sent Christmas cards to Seattle up until two years ago, when they'd been returned, stamped No Forwarding Address.

Kathy shrugged, her once-beautiful face now lined with tension. "I took a chance you still lived here. Your name's on the mailbox up on the highway, so here we are."

"You've had a baby." Allie opened her arms to the fussing child in the car seat, unhooking her gently from the straps and lifting her out of the car. The infant calmed down immediately, sticking her thumb in her mouth and burrowing her face into Allie's neck.

"Yeah." Kathy seemed nervous, rummaging through her leather bag for cigarettes. She found the pack, shook a cigarette out of it and lit it quickly with a match. Allie noticed Kathy's hands were trembling when she pushed her long blond hair over her shoulder.

Allie was at a loss to know what to do for a minute. "Well, come on into the cabin," she said, trying to sound cheerful. "There's a meat loaf in the oven, and we'll give this little girl a bath before dinner. What's her name, Kathy?"

She had noticed the hesitation before the woman answered. "Shelly."

During dinner, Kathy made it clear she needed a place to stay, effectively wheedling sympathy from her tenderhearted friend. Allie felt sorry for her and her baby. "Stay as long as you want." She explained briefly about Paul. "The boys and I have the house to ourselves now." She knew she was being used, but she didn't care. It was so good to have another adult in the house. After she fixed up the tiny spare room with a mattress on the floor for

Kathy and Glen's wicker bassinet for the baby, Allie bathed Shelly and tucked her into bed. As Allie helped Kathy unpack, she looked at the baby and carefully asked, "What about her father?"

"I don't know who he was," Kathy snapped, and left the room.

Throughout the months that followed, Kathy's behavior became more and more irrational. She was gone for hours at a time, often late into the night. Allie watched and worried, fearful to talk to her friend and jeopardize Shelly's welfare. So Allie kept quiet, and happily assumed responsibility for the care of the tiny baby. The little girl became attached to Allie quickly, and there was nothing to complain about. The child rarely napped, but her wide eyes watched everything around her. She didn't like to ride in the car, and she demanded her feedings on schedule, but otherwise was content to be held and pampered—preferably while watching Dan and Glen's every move.

One afternoon near Thanksgiving Kathy chattered excitedly, grabbing the car keys on her way out the door. "I'm trading the Volvo for a van! I've met someone—just east of here, in Montana, and I won't involve you 'cause I know you don't approve, but take care of the kid for me. You're a better mother anyway, and at least I'm the one with the control now. . . ."

Allie hadn't understood that last remark. But she agreed to take care of Shelly for her. It was a labor of love.

Two weeks later, when Allie read in the newspaper that a woman had drowned when her van went out of control on a bridge near the Canadian border, Allie cried. She knew who the victim had to be, although no name was printed in the article. But she waited through the long winter, hoping it was all a mistake and Kathy would return. And in the spring, when the chance came to sell the cabin, she packed up the three children and found an affordable house in the quiet little town of Hope. She liked having neighbors; she needed to reach out and make friends. She was ready to start over again. Without Paul. Without Kathy. And with the new addition to the family, who was struggling to learn to walk. Kathy had called her Shelly, but Glen, remnants of his baby lisp remaining, couldn't pronounce the name. So she had become Sherry instead. Michael Rhodes's missing daughter.

ALLIE'S FIRST REACTION as she lay on her bed Sunday evening was to tell herself it couldn't be true. But it was. Sherry was someone else's child. True, she hadn't known anything about Sherry's father. She had believed Kathy, but she should have known better. Kathy had been an accomplished liar, almost seeming to have more than one personality at times. But to have taken her baby away from the father who loved her . . . That was unforgivable.

But Sherry is my daughter, too, she wanted to cry. I've loved her, taken care of her, been a mother to her for almost three years. She hadn't known her true birth date so she had picked a day in June and had birthday parties. She'd sewed little dresses for her and poured medicine into her when she was sick. How could she give her up?

Maybe he would want all of them. Four for the price of one—a real bargain. That was a laugh. Her own husband hadn't even wanted them, and he'd been in on the production. Why would a relative stranger want to take over the job? A little voice quavered, Because he loves you?

No, Allie thought dejectedly, he had never told her that. But she loved him, and that love couldn't bear the weight of deception. She had to go to him and tell him the truth.

She would tell him his daughter was alive. And she would tell him how much she loved him.

With that resolved, the nervous tremors in her stomach calmed, and she fell asleep.

When she woke, it was barely daylight. The clock on the nightstand blinked 5:02. It was Monday morning, she realized, and wondered at the tension gripping her. She swallowed hard. It had not been just a bad dream. Reality washed in with the cool breeze from the window by the bed.

Allie took a quick shower, then slipped on jeans and a long-sleeved shirt. It was still too cool for shorts, and clouds coated yesterday's blue sky. She crept quietly downstairs before realizing the children weren't home. She shivered, hoping the boys had been warm enough in Barbara's tent. She began to make a fresh pot of coffee. She would sit on the deck, she decided, and use the quiet time to gather together her thoughts.

The back door creaked open, and Allie turned expectantly, a soft smile greeting the man who entered the kitchen. The door shut quietly behind him as he came to her. His arms enveloped her in a hug.

"Mmm . . . this is better than jogging," he murmured, nuzzling Allie's neck, tickling the edge of her shirt.

She loved the solid warmth of him. She was relieved to see him smile so easily after last night's painful conversation. "Jogging already this morning? I thought you had enough exercise yesterday," she teased.

"Uh-uh. The streets are safe. I'm saving my energy for you." He chuckled lightly, wrapping her closer to him.

She could feel him hard against her. "You, uh, have a lot of . . . energy this morning."

He laughed, and slipped his hands over her denim-clad bottom.

"If you want coffee," she warned him, "you'd better let me go." But even as she spoke she wrapped her arms around his neck and welcomed his kiss. She couldn't get enough of him. Why did that surprise her every time?

"We'll have coffee—later," he growled.

"We have to talk," she protested. How could she make love to him when she had so much to tell him? There were so many things to say that were terribly important to both of them.

He looked down at her, his eyes dark with passion. "Talk? When we're about to make love for the third—fourth?—time in twenty-four hours?"

"Are you bragging or counting?"

"Either one's better than talking."

"It's serious, Michael."

"We've spent too much valuable time on serious things." His expression matched hers as he examined the earnest expression in her eyes. "Your eyes turn gray when you're sad."

She hugged him to her, to hide the tears she didn't want him to see. "You don't have to go," she whispered, afraid if she spoke any louder it would be a sob.

"C'mon," he said softly, guiding her toward the stairs. "We'll talk later."

COMPLETE CIRCLES, she mused, waking slowly. She'd dreamed of closing circles and happy endings, dreams a result of sleeping in Michael's arms after a long session of lovemaking. She moved her leg under the sheet to rub Michael's rough one, expecting to find him with her. Nothing. That side of the bed wasn't exactly cold, but it was empty, she decided. She stretched her leg as far as she could before giving up.

He would have been sensitive to the children's coming home early, careful to avoid being found asleep with their mother. He was probably downstairs fixing breakfast. She sighed happily. Her life had changed so much this summer, in just a few short weeks. She would never have thought she could fall in love so quickly. But she had, and she refused to acknowledge the underlying rope of tension coiled in her stomach.

Everything would be all right. It just had to be. The little "what ifs" that whispered threateningly inside her head, she ignored. She pulled on her clothes and hurried downstairs. It was time to tell him the truth.

The kitchen was empty, but Allie smelled coffee. On the counter a piece of paper was propped against her favorite coffee cup. She opened it quickly, reading the unfamiliar slanted scrawl. "Thought it would be better this way. Love, M." She realized she'd never seen his handwriting before. It was strong and bold, easy to read. *Too* easy to read, she decided, crumpling the paper in her hand.

Did this mean he'd left? No, she told herself, running outside. She walked past the corner of the house and saw a whitish patch of lawn in place of the orange tent. She ran up to the road. She couldn't have slept very long. Could he have just ridden away?

"Michael?" A little breeze took her voice and wrapped it around the trees until it returned to her as a pitiful whisper. "Michael?" she tried again. The street was empty. From somewhere nearby a lawn mower roared. Roady, still heavy with unborn kittens, brushed against Allie's leg and mewed. Allie bent down and absently stroked the cat's head. Should she follow him, bring him home, tell him the truth? He couldn't be very far away. There was only one road east. He would have had to get his bike from Bob's garage, pack his things, buy supplies.

But he had told her he wanted to see where his wife and daughter had died. It was important to him, she knew. He had loved Kathy enough to marry her and had hated her for taking his child. Maybe he needed to forgive her. Maybe he needed the time alone.

Allie was stricken with guilt. Michael had ridden away still thinking his daughter was dead, refusing any hope that Will Wentworth offered in contrast. She didn't want Michael hurt any more than he had been already.

She heard the phone ringing through the open kitchen door and hurried inside to answer it, hoping she would hear Michael's voice.

"Hello?" she panted.

"Allie? Did I wake you up?" It was Barbara.

"No, of course not. Are you ready to send the kids home?" She tried to keep the disappointment out of her voice.

"Not yet, but I was worried about you."

"Why?" Did her voice sound so transparent?

"Michael was here earlier, to say goodbye to the children," she explained.

"How long ago?"

"A couple of hours, maybe. He told me you were sleeping, so I decided not to call right away."

"How did the kids take it?" They had grown so used to having Michael around.

"I'm not sure what he told them, but there were lots of hugs. They were all outside playing—heaven only knows what time they woke up this morning—and having kids here to play with took their minds off it. They seem fine."

"Good." Allie was relieved. Four people upset would have been hard to take. She could barely deal with her own misery.

"Allie? Is he coming back?"

The sixty-four-thousand-dollar question. "I don't know, Barb, I just don't know. He left a note, but it didn't say much. He had something important to do in Montana."

Barbara sighed. "I'm sorry, Al. I thought things might have become, well, different for the two of you. I've watched him, the way he looks at you . . . I never would have left you two alone on the island if I'd thought he would leave like this."

"It doesn't matter," Allie assured her, but they both knew it did. "After all, he could be back."

"True," said Barb, her voice brightening. "Keep the faith, look on the bright side and all that."

"I will. And do me a favor? Another one?"

"Sure."

"Give me another hour without the kids, then send them home. I think I need some time to get myself together. Thanks for helping me out so much."

"You're welcome. Besides, you've supplied Tina with enough baby-sitting money to buy her winter wardrobe." Barbara laughed, then her voice became serious. "I really thought I was contributing to a wonderful romance."

"You did," Allie told her, remembering the closeness she and Michael had shared. There was a bond between them, and somehow she'd find him and tell him a three-year-old story. "I know I'll see him again."

IT RAINED for three days. By Thursday Allie thought she would tear out her hair, just to have something to do besides agonize over Michael's whereabouts. She worried about him riding on curving mountain roads, dealing with wet pavement and poor visibility while she paced back and forth in front of rain-sheeted windows. The cat disappeared, worrying the children and making them cranky when their mother forbade them to search for hidden kittens.

Desperate, Allie drove to the Hope Market to rent a video recorder and movies. She met Barbara in front of the movie shelf.

"You look terrible," Barbara stated, frowning.

"I know. But I figure a Sara Lee cheesecake will cheer me up. I'm going to buy two or three." She tried to laugh, but it didn't work.

Barbara arched an eyebrow. "And movies, too? What are you getting?"

Allie studied the rack of movie titles. "Do you think *Night of the Bloody Scream* will keep the kids occupied?"

Barbara laughed. "They'll be occupied all right—with nightmares. How about *Lassie* or *Dumbo*?"

"Danny's in a bloodthirsty stage and thinks any other kind of movie is 'dumb.'" She selected some Walt Disney cartoons. "I think we need a little humor in the house."

Barbara lowered her voice. "Any word from Michael?"

Sadness clouded Allie's eyes. "No. I've been hoping he'd call, but he hasn't."

"This may not be any of my business, but why don't you just go after him?"

"I can't," she replied miserably. "There's more to this than you know."

"Look," Barbara said, smiling. "Put the kids in front of a movie and I'll come over. We can grab a couple of forks and talk our way through the cheesecake. Okay?"

"I think that's the best idea I've heard all day," Allie agreed. It was time to confide in a friend.

Later, while *Superman III* blared from the television set, Allie told an engrossed Barbara the story she'd kept quiet all these years. When she was finished, they sat quietly at the kitchen, a half-empty foil pie plate between them.

Barbara lit a cigarette, blowing smoke toward the ceiling. "You mean all this time he's thought his child was dead?"

Allie pushed aside her plate. "Until last winter, when someone from Montana contacted him. Michael wanted to talk to him, but really didn't have any hope."

"And you think Sherry and Katie are one and the same?"

"I'm sure of it. Kathy just told me a different name, actually Shelly for Michelle, her middle name. Glen just pronounced it funny and the nickname stuck."

"Why didn't you turn her over to the authorities when you thought Kathy was dead? They might have been able to trace the family."

"I tried," Allie said. "I called some hospitals in Portland and Eugene, but either they wouldn't give out information or they didn't have anyone listed by that name. I didn't know then that Kathy had been married or even what day Sherry was born."

"Health and Welfare could have helped you."

"Or put that child into foster care." Allie frowned, shaking her head. "There was no way I was going to put the child through that. I couldn't send her away, knowing there was a chance she might be moved around from home to home for the rest of her childhood. I would have adopted her, but I didn't want to take the chance of being turned down. And Kathy didn't have any family, at least none that I knew of. Besides," she sighed, "that sweet little baby had been with us for months. I *felt* like her mother."

"And you didn't tell Michael." Barbara's eyes were worried as she looked at her friend.

"I was going to, but he left while I was asleep." She grimaced. "Believe it or not, I thought we could be one big happy family."

Barbara leaned forward, resting her elbows on the table. "You can talk to him when he comes back. If he doesn't come back, then you'll know he never really cared."

"That doesn't sound fair. Like punishing him for not loving me," Allie replied.

"Then help him. Drive up to Troy. Find him. Before it's too late." Barbara stubbed out her cigarette in the ashtray. "It sure beats waiting around here feeling miserable."

Miserable was a good description of the situation, Allie thought, sitting in bed that night and finishing the last of the cheesecake. Why shouldn't she go to him, she wondered. It wouldn't be hard to find him in such a small town. She would call Tina to watch the kids again. If she left early in the morning, she planned, she would only have to be gone one day.

The next day, when she kissed the children goodbye, Dan asked solemnly, "Mom, are we ever going to see Michael again?"

"I hope so, honey," his mother sighed, hugging the boy tightly.

"Do you think he'll come to our house again?"

"I don't know. If I see him I'll ask him." She hugged Glen and Sherry, gave Tina instructions for dinner and, laughing, pried the truck's keys from Glen's clutched fingers, hidden behind the child's back. "Caught you!"

Dan followed her to the door. "Tell him I said hi."

"I will. I promise."

Promises, she thought, guiding the jouncing truck east along the narrow two-lane road. There were all kinds of promises. She'd promised Kathy to take care of her daughter. And yet, when she and Michael had made love, that had been a promise, too. An unspoken one that said "I won't hurt you." But she had, even if she hadn't known how.

Michael had been gone four days. He could be on his way back to Hope, Allie figured, so she drove slowly, watching for a cyclist heading in the opposite direction. The road was wet and the whooshing of the tires drowned out what little radio reception there was.

Allie took the Bull River Road north to Troy, where she asked at two motels for Michael Rhodes. He hadn't been to either one. She stopped for lunch before driving toward Yaak. The winding road made her nervous. Fog hung heavily below the trees, leaving Allie with the eerie impression she was all alone in the world. It was as if Michael had disappeared.

The bridge where Kathy had crashed into the river looked harmless, but Allie shivered when she drove over it. She wondered when Michael had been there and how he'd felt when he'd seen it. She wished she could have been with him. She drove on, checking at motels when she arrived in town. Two refused to give out any information.

Another had no record of Michael having been there. By late afternoon Allie was cold, tired and out of ideas. There was no place to go but home.

Exhausted and depressed, she finally arrived in Hope, pulling the truck into the driveway with a shaky sigh of relief. Her neck and shoulders ached from the strain of steering the truck through the misty darkness. Rain fell lightly, mingling with Allie's tears of disappointment as she walked toward the house. Now there was nothing left to do but wait, and pray Michael would return.

During the weekend Allie dragged her sewing machine back to the oak table and halfheartedly assembled quilt blocks for pillows, but the continuing rain made it hard to concentrate. She baked cookies with Sherry and helped the boys build a "fort" with blankets and chairs.

"Mom, is it ever going to be summer again?" Glen whined.

Allie looked out the sliding glass door to the deck, where rain dripped from the roof into the cracks between the boards. "Sure it is," she replied, sounding more certain than she felt.

Monday morning Tina knocked on the door, chattering nonstop while removing her wet coat and sneakers at the back door. "Mom sent me. She took the boys to town and I didn't want to go. This weather's driving us all crazy. Daddy said he was glad to go to work today. Do you mind if I stay here for a while?"

"Of course not." Allie silently blessed Barbara for sending the exuberant teenager. "It's nice to see a different face around here."

"Well, I thought Sherry and I could do some girl stuff," Tina offered. "No charge."

"Sounds like a good deal to me." With the boys down the street playing with the neighbor's visiting grandchildren, she might even have some quiet moments to cut the material for the new quilt. "Sherry's upstairs getting dressed."

"Okay." Tina happily headed up the stairs.

Allie returned to the living room and began to sort through the material she'd stacked on the floor earlier. Tina turned on the radio upstairs and rock music filled the house with an abrasive cheerness. Allie was soon engrossed in designing a quilt ordered at the craft show.

The banging on the sliding glass door surprised her. She didn't expect the boys home so soon. But the eyes that met hers under a rain-soaked yellow slicker were Michael's. His expression was serious, as if he was unsure of his welcome. She hurried to unlock the door, but he shook his head, shouting, "I'm too wet," and headed around the house to the back.

Allie's heart pounded with happiness as she ran to the door to meet him. He leaned his bike against the house and came into the kitchen. "Lady, do you have a place for me to stay? The campground was full," he teased, carefully removing the raincoat. His dark head was wet, drops of rainwater running down his forehead.

She took his coat, her eyes shining. "I think I can make room for one more. I'll hang this by the wood stove. I have a fire going." But she didn't move. She just wanted to look at him. "I didn't think you were coming back. You've been gone for seven days."

"And three hours and forty-two minutes." He grinned. "I was gone longer than I planned." And, he realized as he looked down into Allie's face, he'd been gone longer than he ever should have been.

She took another look at his face. He looked paler somehow, as if dark Montana trees had hidden the sun from him. "Come on into the living room where it's warm."

Michael followed her, watching as she draped the coat by the stove, letting the water drip onto the brick hearth. Why had he worried so much about returning?

Allie watched him tug off his damp sweatshirt and place it on the bricks. The green T-shirt was achingly familiar to Allie, and she longed to touch him, but was unsure what to do. The truth hung between them, dark and heavy, and she knew she had to talk to him.

He reached for her. "Lord, I missed you." He wrapped her in his arms and she felt safe for the first time all week. "Where is everybody?" he whispered. "And who's playing Bruce Springsteen?"

His breath sent little shivers down her neck. "Your lips are cold. So is your face," she murmured. "Tina's upstairs keeping—" she hesitated over the name "—Sherry busy, and the boys are playing with friends down the street."

"Now *I* have somebody to play with." He rubbed his damp cheek against hers. She felt so good against him. "Want to warm me up? We could take a shower together."

She laughed softly, a warm glow spreading through her at the thought of loving Michael in the shower. "I'm not the one who's cold." She pulled away to look at him.

He sighed, pretending to be disappointed. "I guess I can wait." He pulled her back to him and kissed her, hard. "I've missed the feel of you," he murmured. "I think I'm warming up now." He held her hand, unwilling to break contact with her.

"Tell me about the trip," she demanded gently. She pulled him toward the couch where they sat facing each other, hands clasped. She knew she had to tell him, but didn't know how to begin.

His hand tightened around hers and the lines in his face deepened. "It wasn't what I expected."

"What happened?"

"Nothing." He laughed, a harsh dry sound that knifed right into Allie's heart.

"Did you see the bridge?"

He nodded. "It was just a bridge. Easy to see how someone could drive off it." Easy to see death in the shadows.

She knew what it looked like, but she didn't tell him she had looked for him. "Why were you gone so long?"

"I spent some time with Wentworth. He's a nice old man, but he couldn't prove anything. But I enjoyed visiting with him," he said. "He even took me fishing." He tried to smile. "Besides, I needed the time to think. Before I came back here."

She couldn't let him go on. "Michael, we need to talk."

"I know," he agreed wearily, releasing her hand. "But I'd like to have that shower first, get out of these wet clothes and wrap up in one of your quilts."

Footsteps running through the kitchen cut off his words, and Sherry ran in, dressed in a bright pink ruffled gown. Her hair was wound on top of her head, makeup shone from her face, and jewelry dangled from her ears, wrists and neck.

"Mommy! Michael! How do I look?" She was more interested in Michael's reaction than the realization he was back.

Tina followed her into the room, giggling. "She got into your jewelry box before I could stop her. I wouldn't let her wear the high heels down the stairs."

"Where did you get that beautiful outfit?" Michael asked the preening child.

Allie answered for her. "A yard sale. That's a fifty-cent bargain."

Sherry moved delicately in front of the couch and turned around in a circle to show off her hairdo.

"Very beautiful," he told her, trying to keep a straight face.

Sherry climbed onto his lap. "See my earrings?" She dangled the turquoise clips under his nose, tilting her head toward him. He reached out and ran a finger along the delicate gold chain encircling her neck until he brushed two twinkling stones entwined in a golden rose. He stared at Sherry's face for a long moment.

"Pretty?" she asked, and kissed his nose.

His face seemed to turn to granite and his eyes grew dark with an expression Allie couldn't read. "It can't be," he choked, staring at the child's face. He swiveled toward Allie. "Where did you get this necklace?"

Allie sat frozen, not knowing what to say or where to begin. She had forgotten about the necklace. Kathy had left it in a dresser drawer, and Allie had tucked it away, saving it for the time when Sherry was old enough to learn the truth about her mother.

Her silence told him what she couldn't seem to find words for. "How long?" he demanded, color draining from his face.

Allie's stomach tightened. She knew what he asked. "Almost three years. Since October."

"You knew?" His voice held a tone of disbelief. "And you didn't tell me?" Sherry's eyes widened and she grew quiet on Michael's lap. He noticed her stillness the same moment Allie became aware of the child's listening.

"Yes." The word shattered into the silence like a teacup breaking on a stone floor.

His lips tightened and he touched Sherry's wispy hair before the child jumped off his lap. "I wondered why she didn't look like you. I figured your husband was dark, like me. But the face looks like her—" mother was a word that choked him and it certainly didn't apply to the woman who took his infant daughter away from him.

Allie swallowed hard, trying to control her tears. "Sherry, you and Tina go have some more fun upstairs, okay?"

When the girls were out of the room she tried to explain to Michael. "This wasn't the way I planned it. I wanted to tell you myself." She stood up, unable to sit still. What was he thinking? His eyes were filled with pain. The intense look on his face as he watched her seemed to bar any explanations she had to give. "Please believe me, I didn't want it to happen this way. I wanted to tell you, but you had already left."

"I think you could have managed to catch up with me."

It was the stunned expression in his eyes that kept her from telling him she had done just that. The chill in the room froze any answers she could give him. She rubbed her arms, trying to restore the circulation in her chilled body, and watched helplessly as Michael grabbed his raincoat and left the room. Tears coursed down her cheeks as she heard the back door close.

STANDING OUTSIDE in the rain, Michael welcomed the coolness on his face and tried to clear his reeling head. *She's alive.* How could he believe it was true? No, he thought, walking up the steps to the rain-slicked street, she was alive and healthy and beautiful. He took deep breaths, gulping in the moist air as he walked. He felt lighter somehow. He'd grown so used to the heaviness of grief and guilt these past years, and suddenly it was gone. Relief merged with a flaming anger. He'd missed so much of his daughter's life because of a lying woman. No. Make that *two* women, he thought. He knew why Kathy had wanted to hurt him, but he'd be damned if he understood why Allie had helped her. Michael hunched his shoulders against the rain and kept walking as the sky darkened. He'd found his daughter, a child he'd believed dead. It would be a long time before he could trust this strange new feeling of happiness.

IT WAS DARK before Michael returned. Allie had been waiting for him, trying to pretend nothing was wrong. The boys had asked eighteen or twenty times where Michael was after Sherry told them he was back.

"He had errands to do," she'd told them. "He'll be back later." This time she was certain. She finally tucked all three children into bed. She had just finished adding more wood to the fire when she heard him enter the room.

She closed the stove door and stood slowly. There was so much he didn't understand, and by the strained look on his face she could see how frustrated he felt. She hadn't wanted this kind of confrontation. She had to make him understand what really happened. "When Kathy came with Sherry—"

"Her name is Katie," he interrupted. He stood in the middle of the room watching her carefully. "And I gave that birthstone necklace to Kathy the day she gave birth to our daughter."

Allie went over to the couch and sat there, leaning forward. "I didn't know that until you told me," she apologized. "Kathy called her Shelly and Glen couldn't pronounce *l*s."

"Go on."

"I didn't live here then. We lived just on the other side of the Montana-Idaho border, right on the river. My husband had just left the month before, then Kathy arrived. I hadn't seen her in years, but I'd tried to keep in touch. She had a baby with her, but she wasn't exactly a—devoted mother."

"I know." Michael looked out the window into the darkness. "How did you know her?"

"We were in the same foster home." She wished he could turn around so she could read his expression. "Michael, why don't you sit down?"

He ignored her plea, but turned to look at her. "I guessed that, when I was walking. What's hard to understand is how you and Kathy could have been friends."

"Or how you and Kathy could have been married?" she shot back. There was no satisfaction in seeing him wince.

"The kids are asleep, aren't they?" His voice was quiet as he changed the direction of the conversation. "I don't want to upset them." He came closer to where Allie was seated on the couch, but did not sit down. "Why did Kathy come to you?"

Allie thought about that for a moment, trying to find the words to explain a friendship between two teenage girls thrown together in a foster home. "We were always able to talk to each other. She did most of the talking and I did a lot of listening in those days. There was a bond between us," she said, "because she needed me. And God knows," she shivered, remembering, "*I* needed to have someone to take care of, just so I wouldn't have to face the fact that nobody was taking care of me." She laughed, but there was no joy in the sound. "Some childhood, huh?"

"But what kind of childhood was Kathy going to give our daughter?"

"I can't answer that, Michael. They stayed for several months, and I was glad for the company. Kathy seemed, well, wilder than I remembered, but at least she was another adult voice in the house."

He sighed. "Then what?"

"She left Sh—Katie here. She traded her car for a van and said she had—met someone."

He frowned. He didn't know how much more he could bear to hear. "Who? Did you know him?"

Allie curled into the couch cushion. She was starting to feel as if she was on a witness stand. "No. She went out a lot, to the bars."

"How did you know Kathy was dead?" He couldn't help it. The questions shot out like bullets and he felt as shattered as Allie when they hit their target.

"I read it in the paper. Her name wasn't mentioned, but I had a feeling. And she never came back for her baby." Allie stared at the man standing in front of her. It was as if she had never seen him before. "Michael, why are you treating me this way?"

Bull's-eye. His laugh was harsh. "You've had my daughter for three years while I thought she was dead, and you're asking me why I'm treating you this way? I just need some answers, some way to make sense out of something that happened years ago." He ran one hand through his damp hair and absently rubbed the back of his neck. But his voice was kinder when he continued, "Why didn't you tell the police about the baby?"

"I didn't know Kathy was married."

He stepped closer to her. "You think I'm going to believe that?"

"It's the truth," Allie insisted. She wished he would hold her. Or she could hold him. He looked so tired. "Why would I want to keep a child from her father?" She clasped her hands tightly in her lap. She didn't know how much more of this she could take. "Michael, please—"

He turned. "Please, what? What kind of fool do you think I am?"

She rose and went to him. "I don't think you're a fool." She touched his arm and said softly, "I didn't know who Sherry was until you told me. And then you left."

He pulled away from her touch. "You let me go."

"I went after you, but I couldn't find you." She stared at the place on his arm where she had touched him.

He shrugged. "That's easy to say."

"No, it's true." She gazed up at him, willing him to look at her and believe what she said. "I would never have kept Sherry if I'd known she had a father. Kathy told me she didn't know who the father was. I knew she didn't have any family, and I'd promised Kathy I'd take care of her baby."

"How were you going to get her a birth certificate?" he asked wearily. "How were you planning to register her for school? You can't just make up these things, you know."

She shrugged. "It didn't seem important then. Not when there was a sweet little baby who didn't have anyone in the world but me." *And I loved her so much*, she added silently.

He deliberately walked away from her. "She has a father now." Father. He was going to be a damn good one, too.

"Yes."

"I'm going to take her home. Where she belongs." He stood in the doorway. "We'll try to catch a plane out of Spokane tomorrow. I'll help you pack her things in the morning. She won't need much. I'll buy her whatever she needs when we get to Portland."

"Please, don't do this," she cried.

"I'm sorry, Allie, but this time I'm keeping my child."

Her eyes filled with tears. "I never meant to hurt anyone. Especially you."

He sighed, his eyes dark as he stood in the shadows. "And I don't want to hurt you, either. But there just doesn't seem to be any choice."

She didn't know what to say. She realized his anger and pain were years old, a current connecting the past with the present. The happy ending she'd envisioned for all of them washed away, erased by the despair that filled the room.

HELPLESSNESS gripped Allie Tuesday morning as she watched Michael prepare to leave. She ached to tell him the entire story but each time she approached he turned away. He believed he had been deceived again, and Allie realized there wasn't anything more she could say to make a difference. She had no legal rights to the child and no hope of winning a court battle. And she wouldn't have dragged Sherry through that anyway.

Numb with heartache, Allie sorted through the clothes in her daughter's dresser drawers, determined to make this as easy as possible for Sherry. She selected what outfits Sherry would need right away and stacked them into a small pile for the suitcase. She would let Sherry decide what toys scattered throughout the cluttered room she wanted to take with her. The favorites changed from week to week. Allie could mail her the rest.

"I want my Rosie," said Sherry, demanding her favorite teddy bear be packed.

"Okay." Allie remembered the birthday party last June when the boys had given the stuffed animal to their sister.

"You come, too?" Sherry crawled onto the bed and clutched Rosie.

"Not this time, honey. But the boys and I will stay here and feed Roady and take care of the kittens for you." Dan and Glen had found Roady's hiding place early that morning and had decided not to move the three tiny kittens to the playhouse until they were older.

"Can I take one?"

"They're not old enough to leave their mommy yet." A sob threatened Allie's words. She cleared her throat and blinked back the tears. Sherry wasn't old enough to leave her mother, either. What on earth was Michael doing?

"Oh." The child was silent for a minute. "Where I going?"

"I thought Michael and I told you." Allie's heart contracted painfully as she remembered Michael's explanations to the three children this morning. He had been sensitive to their feelings and had answered questions patiently.

Sherry nodded. "But I can't 'member."

"He was your daddy a long time ago when you were still a tiny baby." Allie held up her hands to show her the size. "Then he lost you and was very sad. Until he found you here with a new mommy and two new brothers."

"Yeah, Sherry," said Dan, appearing in the doorway. "And now you get to ride in an airplane." His voice turned wistful. "I've never even done that."

"'Kay," she sighed, her face still clouded with uncertainty.

To comfort her, Allie said, "You'll have fun. And you can take all your dolls, too. I'll box them up and they can go on the plane with you." Allie began to load the suitcase with Sherry's belongings. "Why don't you go see the kitties again? But remember, you can't touch them."

"'Kay." The little girl scampered out of the room.

Glen joined Danny in the doorway. "It's not fair." Glen sniffed. "She gets to go and we don't."

Allie tucked the forgotten bear in the suitcase and snapped it shut. "We'll go, too, one of these days. I promise." Those damn promises again. She looked over at the boys. Dan looked relieved.

"Really?" Glen asked.

"Cross my heart," she told them. And she meant it. She could still visit the child she considered a daughter. And the boys could see their sister. Surely she and Michael could work something out.

She told herself that over and over again as the morning continued. She pretended it was a normal day for the sake of the children. If she acted as if there was nothing unusual in what was happening maybe the kids wouldn't be upset. She would have liked to confide in Barbara or Jeanne, but she decided against that. She couldn't tell anyone what was going on, as if that would make it real. She would have to get through this day alone. Allie knew if she lost control of the iron strength she held on to so tightly she would probably collapse into a sobbing heap.

"We're ready," Michael announced from downstairs.

She went to the top of the stairs. "So soon?" she called.

"I think it's best." He looked tired, and Allie wondered if he'd lain awake all night on the living room couch.

"Dan, carry that suitcase down for me, please." Allie went into the bathroom and locked the door. She splashed cold water on her face and rubbed her skin dry with a towel. Her eyes were a dull khaki color as she looked at herself in the mirror. *Just get through the next part,* she told herself. *You can do it.*

When she entered the kitchen a few minutes later, she felt stronger and hoped she would not fall apart in front of the children. She wanted to beg Michael not to do this, but she couldn't find the words. His face was drawn; he looked as miserable as she felt. Michael watched Sherry constantly, as if he couldn't believe she was real.

"It's time for us to go," he told the child.

"What 'bout you, Mommy?" asked Sherry. "You come, too?"

Allie didn't know how to respond. She didn't believe in lying to her children, but she didn't want to hurt them, either.

She looked up at Michael, her heart in her eyes. He watched her steadily, but there was no clue to his feelings in those dark eyes. Tiny flickers of anger seared through her pain as she defiantly replied, "Sooner than you think honey. You need to spend some special time alone with your daddy first, okay?"

The little girl smiled importantly. "And Grandma and Grandpa, too."

"Yes. I know. Aren't you the lucky duck?" Allie knelt down and hugged her tightly. "You be a good girl on the bus and the airplane." And she whispered, "Make sure to go to the bathroom whenever you have to."

"'Kay." Sherry's lower lip quivered slightly. Her pudgy hands clung on to Allie's neck. Allie hugged her again. Then, afraid to transpose her grief onto the sensitive child, she gently unwrapped Sherry's arms and kissed the tiny palms. "You be a good girl in Oregon and make me very proud of you."

Sherry nodded, tears glistening in her eyes. She went to hug the boys. Normally Glen wouldn't have let a girl near him, but today he tolerated Sherry's embrace. Danny hugged the little girl quickly, a stubborn expression on his freckled face.

Michael walked over to the boys, who didn't quite know what to make of his new relationship with their family. "I wish you could come, too," he told them.

Over my dead body, Allie thought. She bit her lip before voicing her feelings out loud. She stood helplessly in the middle of the kitchen watching a scene she was unable to stop.

"You don't want us," Danny sneered. "But don't worry," he told the stricken man. "We're used to it." He took Glen by the shoulder. "C'mon. Let's get out of here."

Michael touched Dan's arm, wishing he could erase the bitter look on the boy's face. "I'd like to leave my bike here."

Danny frowned. "Why?"

"Just because," he said lamely. His face grew taut. "Because I'd like to know you were using it. Glen's too small for it now, but it could be yours until you could both share it. What do you say?" *C'mon, Dan, you're killing me.*

Danny was clearly astounded by the gift, but his anger over Michael's upsetting the family was still in his face. "No, thanks."

Allie intervened. "We'll ship it to you," she offered, having no intention of doing so, but wanting to save Danny any more heartache. She'd ship it all right. But she'd back the truck over it a few times first.

"Don't bother," Michael said. He never wanted to see the damn thing again.

"Fine."

The boys ran upstairs, but Allie knew they'd be watching out the bedroom window. Michael picked up Sherry's suitcase and the cardboard box of toys. He slung a nylon pack over his shoulder. "I left the tent in the garage. If the boys want it, they can have it."

She refused to thank him. "This isn't the end, you know." Her glance flickered pointedly to Sherry. She couldn't say anything more without disturbing the child, but he would know what she meant.

"For now it has to be." He sighed. "We've been all through this. You have no rights."

"Love doesn't count?"

His jaw tensed. "It never has before."

She reached out to touch his arm, her pleading gaze locked with his. "I am not your ex-wife. Please don't punish me for what she did to you."

"I can't help that right now. I just want to take my daughter home." He turned away from the stricken woman, unable to face the pain in her eyes. "C'mon, babe," he said to his daughter. "Let's go." He took her hand gently as they walked to the door.

Sherry began to cry quietly, and Allie clung to control as the child hesitated. "Mommy?"

Allie's voice was rough and strained. "You go on now. I'll see you soon."

The door slammed behind them. Allie stood frozen in the middle of the kitchen as the shock of what had just taken place made a barrier to all feeling. She watched as the man and child walked up the cement steps, on their way to the Hope store where a bus to Spokane came through twice a day. Michael must have called to find out the times.

When they disappeared from her sight, Allie trudged upstairs. The emptiness in the house was a sword slicing through the disbelief. Sherry's room was a disaster of strewn clothes and an unmade bed. The cartoon-character sheets were a riotous jumble of color and it hurt Allie's eyes to look at them. She shut the door. She would deal with cleaning the room later when she could bear to believe her daughter was really gone. But it would always be Sherry's room. Or Katie's. Would Michael change her name?

I never wanted to hurt anybody. She sighed to herself. *I love them both.* Why wouldn't he understand?

She heard the boys whispering furiously in their room. "Knock, knock," she said to the closed door.

"Come in, Mom," Dan called.

A fierce protectiveness gripped Allie at the sight of her two sons. Dan sat on the floor beside Glen's bed. Glen had tucked himself under the covers and his eyelids were red. He held a wad of damp toilet paper in his hand.

"Are you sad, too?" Allie asked carefully. Glen had been so quiet today, but his green eyes had seen everything. *He must be more confused than I am,* Allie thought.

"Yeah," he said with a sniff. "And I don't feel so good."

He was pale and his brown hair hung limply on his forehead. Allie felt his cheek with the back of her hand. "You're not hot. Are you very tired?"

He nodded. "Sort of."

"Why don't you just close your eyes for a while?" She avoided using the word "nap." She smoothed his forehead soothingly.

"You stay here?" he asked anxiously.

"Sure."

"I'm gonna set up my army men so we can play when you wake up, Glen," Dan offered.

Allie was grateful for her older son's help.

Glen grabbed her hand. "Michael's Sherry's *real* dad?"

Allie nodded. "That's right."

"What about our dad? What if *he* came back?"

Allie thought quickly. "Could he take you away? Is that what you're asking?"

Glen's eyes were wide. "Uh-huh."

Dan came over and sat on the bed beside his mother.

"Your father went away a long time ago," she began, but she wasn't sure what to say. How could she tell the boys their father didn't want to be a father anymore? And yet, they needed reassurance that he wouldn't come and take them away. She took a deep breath and decided it was time for the truth. A little more truth around here couldn't hurt them any more than it had already. "Your father wanted to be free to do a lot of things—adventure stuff—he'd always dreamed of doing. The only trouble was that he had a wife—"

"You," interjected Glen.

"Right," she said, "and a family. It was hard for him to have adventures when he had a family to take care of. So he wasn't very happy." She made herself more comfortable on the bed, trying to recall the freckled face of the young man she had thought she was in love with. Looking back, she realized she had been more in love with the idea of having her own family. Paul was alone in the world, too. And the two of them had struggled to make their marriage work. "So your dad and I decided—" here she stretched the truth, recalling Paul's sudden announcement that he was leaving for Alaska "—that we wouldn't be married anymore. He could go off and have adventures and I would take care of the family, which made us both very happy." Sort of, she added silently.

"He won't come back, will he?" Dan asked.

Since he hadn't written or called in almost four years, Allie didn't think there was much chance of his returning home. "No. I don't think so. But even if he came to see you, he could never, never take you away."

"Oh, good." Glen sighed, closing his eyes. "Cuz I want to stay here with you."

"Of course you do, silly. I'm your mom." She ruffled his hair affectionately and stood up. "I'll be in my room if you need me."

Feeling drained and defenseless, she went into her bedroom and closed the door. She slipped off her jeans and crawled into her bed. Closing her eyes, she thought about all she'd told her sons. Tears made a hot trail past her ears to sink into the pillow. She tried to stop crying, but the vision of Sherry and Michael walking out the door only grew more vivid. Sherry's teary confused expression would haunt her from now on.

And then Michael. She had loved him as she had never loved another man. He had been such a special person in her life, and what had happened? He'd betrayed her by taking her daughter—*his* daughter, she corrected—and leaving. Bitterness choked her and angry sobs burned her throat. The tears continued to pour, hot and salty, until Allie's chest ached. Turning her face into the pillow to muffle her sobs, she wept until falling into an exhausted sleep.

It was after one o'clock when she woke up. The afternoon sun heated the room and the house was quiet. Allie wondered if Glen had slept, too. She went into the bathroom and splashed water on her puffy eyelids and brushed her tangled hair. She didn't want the boys to see any trace of tears. She tiptoed to their room and gently opened the door. Danny's interpretation of World War II was spread all over the floor. He looked up at her and smiled as he made quiet cannon sounds. Glen was asleep, but he looked pale. Something was wrong; he just didn't look well.

"Mom, what's poison ivy look like?"

"Why, Dan?"

"My back itches me."

"Here. Let me see." She bent over him and pulled up his shirt. Several red spots dotted his back. "You feel warm, too," she noted. "Do you itch anywhere else?"

He pulled his shirt down. "Sort of behind my ears."

"I'll be back in a minute." She hurried down to the bookcase in the sewing room to find her child-care manual. She figured she needed some expert help. There was an empty place on the shelf and she looked at it curiously before realizing what was missing.

"Oh, no," she murmured. Sherry's baby book was gone. Michael must have taken it. Her heart broke again. Was he trying to wipe out all the traces of Sherry's presence in this family? Tears for her daughter welled up, but she couldn't think about that now, she reminded herself. She grabbed the thick paperback manual from the shelf and flipped through the index to "rashes." Moments later she had a good idea what was wrong with her sons. But she called Barbara for a second opinion.

"Hey! I was just about to call you," her friend answered. "I've been going crazy wondering what was going on at your house. And Jason came down with chicken pox yesterday."

"You just answered my question," Allie said.

"You, too? Oh, no. Which kid?"

"Both boys, I think. Dan has a rash on his back and Glen fell asleep not feeling well. I'll probably find spots all over him when he wakes up."

"I think they must have caught it from the Matsons' grandchildren," Barbara decided. "The boys were down there a lot. What about Sherry? Is she okay?"

Allie took a deep breath. She supposed she had to tell somebody sometime. "She's not here, Barb. Michael took her to Portland."

There was shocked silence before Barbara asked, "For how long?"

"I don't know. He found out who she was before I could tell him. He just wanted to take her home, he said."

"Oh, Al, I'm so sorry. Tina told me he was back but I was hoping you'd worked it all out by now."

The sympathy in her friend's voice made it hard for Allie to answer. She cleared her throat as tears threatened to well up again. "I think I'm still in shock. They took a bus to Spokane this morning and were going to catch a plane this afternoon."

"He fell in love with you, Allie. He'll be back."

"No. I don't think so." She didn't think she could talk anymore. She took a deep breath. "Look, I'd better go check on the boys again. I'll talk to you later."

"But what about Sherry? She's been exposed to chicken pox. Michael should know. Good heavens—she could be infecting a whole planeload of people and not even know it!"

"You're right," Allie said in a worried tone, "I never thought about that."

"What about you? Have you had it?"

"Oh, sure. When I was a kid. But I wonder about Michael."

"Now there's a man who can take care of himself. You just worry about yourself and the boys. Call me if you need anything. Tina had chicken pox when she was a baby so she can come over if you need to run to the store. You'll need plenty of calamine lotion," she advised.

"Okay. Thanks." She hung up, feeling better after the phone call. At least she was sure what was wrong with the boys. She hoped Sherry and Michael would be okay. Sherry would want her mother if she was sick. What would Michael do then?

The next days were a mixture of cranky children, tepid baths in baking-soda water, strained patience and constant worry. Her doctor assured her she was doing all the right things, but it was frustrating, she thought as she folded another load of clean pajamas and fresh sheets. She had no idea if Sherry was suffering with chicken pox, too. She had no luck trying to get in touch with Michael. His phone number was unlisted. She called several Portland high schools before locating the one where he worked. But she'd

been told he was on a leave of absence and had been refused his phone number. The secretary was kind enough
to give her Michael's home address, but Allie preferred to
call him.

Her next step was to contact his parents, but the oper-
ator said without a first name she could not locate the
telephone number. Her next brilliant idea was to try calling the sporting goods store and ask for Jake. She searched
through her phone bill and found the Oregon number Michael had called the first day he came to her house. "Jake?"
she asked casually. "Is Michael around?" She acted as if
she was an old friend.

"Not this week. Can I help you instead, or give him a
message?"

"Well, I seem to have lost his phone number. I have, uh,
some questions about an order."

His voice sharpened. "What company are you from?"

She took the first name she saw—a can of fruit cocktail
sitting on the kitchen counter. "Western Family."

"I don't seem to know anything about it," Jake replied
cautiously. "Why don't you give me your name and number and I'll get back to you?"

Allie hung up. *Dumb, dumb, dumb,* she cursed herself, throwing the empty can of fruit cocktail into the garbage. *You'll never make a good spy.*

The ache of missing Michael and Sherry grew worse
every day. She wondered if she would ever be able to
function normally again. It even hurt to breathe, as if the
broken pieces of her heart had lodged sideways in her
chest. Allie decided work would help, and spent what
spare time she had on the new quilt. She wrote a letter to
Michael telling him about the chicken pox and suggesting
Sherry see a doctor. She asked him to call her. She told him
she loved him.

She made some decisions, too. The boys were feeling better every day. When the quilt was finished she'd be free to go to Portland. She didn't want to disappoint the people who had ordered it. The deposit they'd given her was a substantial boost to her savings account. She'd sell the truck to one of Tina's friends, a boy who wanted to "mess around with the engine," he'd told her. With the sale of the truck and the money in her savings account she'd have enough to buy a new second-hand car. One of her neighbors had a station wagon for sale, and Allie looked at it longingly every time she saw him drive by her house.

Her new plans kept her busy sewing long into the night again, although this time Michael wasn't there to fix coffee and keep her company. It rained again. The grandchildren who had infected the neighborhood with chicken pox recovered and went home. Jeanne and Bob returned from their honeymoon trip to Canada and were anxious to show Allie the videotape of the wedding. It seemed to Allie that the rest of the world was spinning along normally while her life could be declared a disaster area.

"You look terrible," Barbara said when she and Jeanne stopped in one afternoon.

"Gee, thanks," Allie quipped, trying to smile. "I feel better now that I know that. Come on in and cheer me up some more." She was happy to see her friends.

Barbara peered into the living room. "We came to rescue you from the quilting frame. It definitely looks like you need a break."

"We brought some wine, too," Jeanne offered. "I'll get the glasses while you tell us what you're doing."

Allie sank into the couch. "As soon as the quilt's done and the kids are okay, any day now, we're going to Portland. I want to see Sherry and I'm going to make Michael listen to me no matter how long it takes."

Jeanne handed her a glass of white wine. "Barbara told me what happened. It sounds like that man has really been hurting all these years."

"He has," Allie sighed, "but we have to work something out. Maybe I could have Sherry visit here sometimes."

Barbara chimed in, "Maybe you can marry him."

Allie shook her head. "He made it clear what he thought of me. Any feelings he had were gone the minute he realized I knew Sherry was his daughter and didn't tell him."

"How long has he been gone?" asked Jeanne.

"Almost two weeks now. And I don't even have his phone number. But I've written several times, asking him to call me." She shrugged, feeling helpless. "I don't even know if he's reading my letters."

Barbara examined the creamy ribboned quilt stretched between wooden boards. "This is gorgeous. It looks finished to me."

"Almost. Then I just have some edging to sew on by hand."

"Then what?" Jeanne asked.

"Then I mail it, buy the Lassers' station wagon, sell the truck and head west."

"You sound determined." Barbara looked worried as she looked at Allie. "Are you sure?"

"I'm not going to let anything stop me now."

ALLIE LIFTED the carefully wrapped box from the front seat of the yellow station wagon, checking again to make sure the label was glued on properly. The boys scrambled out of the car, glad to be out of the house. The spots had healed, and though the boys were still pale, they were no longer contagious.

It was a beautiful sunny day. A bright day like the one Allie remembered when she had first seen Michael. She pushed the thought out of her head. She didn't want to question how her life would have been if she hadn't stopped to check her mail that Friday. If the kids hadn't wrestled. If the emergency brake had worked. If, if, if. That little two-letter word could drive her crazy if she let it.

The boys had letters and pictures to mail to Sherry, even though they hoped to see her before the letters arrived.

"Race you to the mailbox!" Dan yelled to Glen.

"C'mon, you guys, open the door for me."

Dan pulled open the heavy glass door, and Allie stepped into the cool darkness of the foyer. She walked over to the counter and set the box down. It was surprising how heavy quilts were. "Hello, Jim!" she called into the empty room.

"Coming!"

When he appeared from the back room, Allie bought stamps for the boys' letters and filled out the necessary forms to insure the quilt. Glen begged to have his hand stamped. The kindly postmaster agreed and stamped the back of Glen's hand, Special Delivery.

"Hold my mail for a few weeks, will you, Jim? We're taking a trip."

"Vacation? Good for you."

I hope so, she thought to herself. "Let's go," she told the boys. "Did you mail the letters?"

"Yeah!" They ran out the door and Allie followed slowly. Her house was locked, the refrigerator was cleaned out, the suitcases were loaded, the quilt was on its way, and the car had a full tank of gas. She'd packed a cooler full of juice, diet cola, sandwiches and cookies. One stop in town at the bank for money, and they'd be on their way.

It would take two days to reach Portland, since she was a slow driver and the boys would need lots of rest stops.

She blinked to adjust to the sunshine. It felt good on her bare arms and legs. She ushered the excited boys past a large motor home that filled the space beside them.

"Okay, kids! This is it!" She hustled them into the back seat and closed the door, then opened her own door and slid behind the wheel. She reached for the key to start the car. It wasn't there. She bent closer to examine the unfamiliar dashboard. No key ring dangled from the steering column where the ignition was located.

"Glen," she said good-naturedly, "where are the keys?" She peered into the rearview mirror at her sons.

"Now you're gonna get it," Dan muttered.

Glen's bewildered green eyes filled with tears. "I didn't take them! Honest!"

"We could give him a lie detector test, Mom," suggested Dan.

"You've been watching too much television." Allie fumbled inside her purse. "Maybe I put them in here." She dumped the contents of her bag onto the ivory vinyl seat while the boys dangled over the seat for a closer look.

"Can I have that gum?"

"Me, too?"

She absently handed them the open pack. "For heaven's sake!" she said, disgusted with herself. Here she thought she had everything so organized and she couldn't even get out of Hope.

"Maybe you left them in the post office, Mom."

"Let's hope you're right, Dan," she said. She returned to the post office, squeezing carefully past the motor home again. Jim told her he hadn't seen any keys on the counter. They checked the floor, and Jim even looked in the mail bin in case Glen had tossed them in there by accident. Jim looked up the phone number for a locksmith in the phone book. She couldn't believe she only had one car key. Her house key was on that key ring, but Barbara had a spare so she could check the house and feed the cats while Allie was gone. She'd have to go back to Barbara's to call the locksmith. This was ridiculous.

She retraced her steps to the car, checking the pavement carefully in case she'd dropped the ring of keys while carrying the box. "Glen? Are you sure you're not playing another trick on me? Cross your heart?"

"No tricks," a deep voice answered behind her. "Cross my heart."

She whirled around. Michael leaned against the white motor home, a ring of keys dangling from his fingers. His tan face creased into a smile as he looked at her. She thought he looked tired.

He thought she looked wonderful.

"What are you doing here?" she gasped. "And where's Sherry?"

"Inside." He gestured toward the motor home. "Showing the boys how everything works."

She wanted to come closer to him to see if he was real, but she was rooted to the pavement. "You're back."

"I know." His expression turned serious.

"But why?" Was he going to hurt her again? Had he forgotten something Sherry needed?

Wishing he could hold her, Michael approached Allie. She looked so suspicious, and he couldn't blame her after what he'd put her through. "I've been doing a lot of thinking. Sherry had the chicken pox—"

"Is she all right?"

He put his hands on her shoulders to reassure her. "She's fine now. Her new grandparents have been spoiling her. The doctor said it was a mild case, but I had to wait until she was well enough to travel. I figured she'd be more comfortable in this thing—" he nodded toward the motor home "—so I borrowed it from my parents."

"But why did you come back?" She had to have an answer before she hoped for too much.

"There's a lot to talk about, Allie. Can we go—" he hesitated before finishing the question "—home?"

She shook her head. "I don't think so. Not yet." She couldn't bear the thought of having Michael in her house, knowing he was going to leave it again.

He was disappointed, but he was going to make her listen to him. "Okay, how about your car? Can we talk there?"

He opened the door to the back seat and she had no choice but to scoot inside. He climbed in beside her and shut the door. "I followed that old blue pickup of yours all the way to the dump before I realized you weren't driving it. The kid who bought it told me you had a yellow wagon. When I found out you weren't home I went over to Barbara's. She told me you were down here mailing a quilt." He sighed with relief. "I'm glad I caught up with you first."

"I'd like to see Sherry."

"In a minute. She really wants to see you, too. She missed you terribly." He took Allie's hand and she tried to remain unresponsive to the warmth of his touch. She wanted to lean against him and feel that he was real. Instead, she moved back to lean against the door.

"You haven't told me why you came back," she insisted.

His low voice was serious. "There have been a lot of things I haven't understood, Allie. When Sherry was sick I went through the baby book you made for her. I wanted to see what shots she'd had and if she'd ever had chicken pox and measles—that sort of thing." He increased the pressure on her hand. "There was an awful lot of love in that book. It took me awhile to realize what it meant."

Allie's eyes filled with tears. "You didn't believe me when I told you the truth of what happened, did you?"

"I do now. And I'm sorry for the pain I've caused you. I should have been on my knees thanking you for taking care of my daughter. If it wasn't for you, she *would* have drowned with Kathy. I know that now. It took me some time to realize that even though I had my daughter back, there was more missing from my life. Sherry needs her mother, Allie, and I don't want to raise her alone." He took a deep breath, watching Allie carefully. "Will you marry me?"

Allie sat stunned. These were words she'd dreamed of hearing from the man she had grown to love. But something was wrong. She shook her head slowly. "No, Michael. I'm not going to marry you to give Sherry a mother."

He started to interrupt.

"Wait," she said. "Hear me out."

He frowned, but was silent.

"I've been Sherry's mother since Kathy died. And, whether you believe it or not, I never knew about you until you told me your story." She paused. "I fell in love with you, Michael. But I won't marry you now." Her voice quavered at the last words, but she hoped he wouldn't notice.

He looked surprised and sad. "What can I say or do to make you change your mind?"

You could tell me you love me, she pleaded silently. "Nothing." The single word was flat with disappointment. She sighed, reluctant to reveal her feelings.

"I'm sorry I hurt you." His voice was formal now. He turned away from her and started to open the car door. "We'll work out some sort of shared custody arrangement for Sherry." He noticed the suitcases in the back of the wagon. "Where are you going?"

"Just getting away for a while," she answered, looking down at her hands.

"To Portland?" he guessed.

She ignored the question. "I'd like to see Sherry now."

"Allie, tell me why you were going to Portland."

"We wanted to see Sherry. I—I wanted to try to explain about Kathy and what happened."

He touched her shoulder, rubbing it gently. "You've taken care of a baby who needed a home. You took me in when you had no choice, and it has come to this."

"I'm no saint, Michael," she protested. She wished he wouldn't touch her. She could break apart any moment now.

"You asked me once if love counted for anything. I hope it does, because I love you very much."

Before Allie could react to his words, he pulled her toward him and kissed her. His lips were warm and broke through the defenses she'd erected to protect herself from being hurt again. She hesitated before she wrapped her arms around his neck. He'd come back. He'd said he loved her. That was all she needed to hear. When he reluctantly ended the kiss, she smiled, her face lighting with happiness. "I love you, Michael."

"Marry me?"

Playful shrieks came from the open windows of the motor home. Allie winced. "Are you sure you know what you're getting into?"

"Yep. I'll adopt yours if you'll adopt mine."

"Deal." She smiled, wiping away the tears of joy and relief.

"Thank God," he groaned, and pulled her to him again.

"Michael," she said, laughing, "everyone in town will be talking about this. There are people coming in and out of the post office. And the kids are probably close to destroying that expensive camper—"

"Hope will get used to us," he insisted. "Would you mind if we lived here? I'd like to open up another branch of the sporting goods store in town."

She nodded wordlessly. There was too much to take in at once.

"C'mon," he said, opening the car door and tugging her hand. "Let's put your suitcases in the motor home, take your car back to the house and go get married." He patted the motor home. "This thing sleeps six." He winked. "There's a private double bed up above. With curtains."

He caught her face between his hands and looked down upon her lovingly. "I'll never hurt you again, Allie. I promise." Then he guided her through the open door of the cab and into the living area where the children chattered excitedly.

Dan and Glen grinned as Sherry climbed up on a couch to stand at eye level with Allie. "See, Mommy? I'm here!" she announced proudly.

Michael stood close behind Allie and she leaned against his strong body. She smoothed the child's hair, smiling into the shining dark eyes that were so much like her father's. "I know, honey. Welcome home."

Harlequin Temptation

COMING NEXT MONTH

Take 4 books & a surprise gift FREE

SPECIAL LIMITED-TIME OFFER

Mail to   **Harlequin Reader Service**®

In the U.S.	In Canada
901 Fuhrmann Blvd.	P.O. Box 609
P.O. Box 1394	Fort Erie, Ontario
Buffalo, N.Y. 14240-1394	L2A 5X3

YES!   Please send me 4 free Harlequin Romance® novels and my free surprise gift. Then send me 8 brand-new novels every month as they come off the presses. Bill me at the low price of $1.99 each*—an 11% saving off the retail price. There are no shipping, handling or other hidden costs. There is no minimum number of books I must purchase. I can always return a shipment and cancel at any time. Even if I never buy another book from Harlequin, the 4 free novels and the surprise gift are mine to keep forever.   118 BPR BP7F

*Plus 89¢ postage and handling per shipment in Canada.

Name _____ (PLEASE PRINT)

Address _____ Apt. No.

City _____ State/Prov. _____ Zip/Postal Code

This offer is limited to one order per household and not valid to present subscribers. Price is subject to change.   DOR-SUB-1D